HER

*Sacrifice*

# HER

## *Sacrifice*

# SUMMER YORK

This is a work of fiction. Names, characters, places, and incidents are products of the authors imagination or are used fictitiously and are not to be construed as real. Any resemblance to actual events, locales, organizations, or persons, living or dead, is entirely coincidental.

First Edition

ISBN: 979-8-9867700-0-0

Fiction/Christian

Fiction/Drama

You're mine, and I am yours.
There's nothing I wouldn't give for you.
Until my last days, until my last breath,
I will sacrifice my life for you.

Summer York

"Let all that you do be done in love."

✻

-1 Corinthians 16:14

# *Chapter 1*

I hate her. She doesn't understand me. She just wants me to be someone else. I just want to get away from her. Sofia thought to herself, as she was storming through the crowded mall to get away from her mother and her endless criticisms about who she is. The further she walked away she could feel her anger build like an ember in the pit of her stomach, and the more she thought about it, the more she fanned the growing flame. Frustrated and entangled in her own thoughts, she could barely hear her mother calling her name in a stern manner. Her voice echoing through the crowd, "SOFIA! SOFIA!"

Instead, she chose to ignore her, and let her thoughts be captivated by anger.

Nearing the door Sofia pushes it open with great force and begins her way to their car. Without a second thought she steps onto the mall crosswalk. Suddenly she feels an instant grab of her arm, and her entire body is thrust backward nearly stealing her breath away.

"Sofia, dear Jesus," her mother cried. Then quickly brought her into a warm embrace, to simply take a moment to breathe her in. Something a mother does as if to reassure themselves that their child is okay, and that all is well. As soon as her mother receives that simple assurance of her daughter's safety, her mind reverts remembering the incident at hand.

"You have to be careful and look both ways! You almost walked in front of that car," she said pulling her away to make eye contact. Desperately attempting to connect with her to get her to understand the severity of the actions made.

Sofia immediately jerked away from her mother in aggravation, instantly feeling the criticism from her mother's voice. "That car didn't hit me; it was nowhere near me," Sofia stated in annoyance. She took a step back as she spoke, attempting to create a level of equality between her and her mother, symbolically trying to suggest that her mother shouldn't speak to her that way.

"Didn't you hear them honk their horn after they passed? Everyone was scared!" her mother tried to explain. Shifting her glance side to side looking to the crowd, she attempted to show her daughter that her reaction was justified.

"I am fine. I didn't need your help," Sofia said. Then stepped to the crosswalk once more first looking both ways, glancing back towards her mother. Feeling like she proved her mother's statements wrong, she stormed off across the way. This time she was determined to make it to the car to save herself from the embarrassment of another one of her mother's over-reactions.

As soon as she made it to the car, she planned to stew inside the vehicle. Regrettably, the doors were locked. With irritation she leaned against it, despite how dirty it was, with arms crossed and waited for her mother to open the doors. Stuck outside the vehicle, she couldn't help but fan the overwhelming thoughts, that on top of everything else, she must wait. All because her overbearing mother wants to make a dramatic scene. Those thoughts elicit a wave of aggravation from Sofia, that could only be let out in a heavy sigh.

Seeing her daughter's frustration, Sofia's mom, unlocked the doors as she walked up hoping it would at least end the scene they were causing. Sofia immediately rushed in slamming the door behind her. Her mother entered the car resting her hands on her steering wheel, releasing a deep breath of air, showing her frustration as well. She took a moment, as she looked at her sullen daughter, and the only question she could manage was, "What is going on with you, Sofia?" she asked.

The question was simple to most, but Sofia could only hear the condescending tone escape her mother's throat, as if she were the awful one. She couldn't bear it any longer, and if her mother wanted so desperately to know what was "*going on*" with her, then she shall hear it all. It was time to unleash her feelings, and all her mother's overbearing, stifling, and judgmental quips were going to stop. Without further hesitation, she let it all out.

"Everything, according to you!" Sofia burst out, revealing her feelings with a sense of empowerment.

"What's that supposed to mean?" returned her mother in a puzzling state.

"Really? You're constantly telling me everything I do is wrong. Every time I make a small mistake you have to point it out!" she began to yell back. "That car didn't even come close to me, you just wanted to embarrass me because I didn't look both ways."

"That car was a foot away from you. Had I not pulled you away, I would be less a daughter," her mother stated trying to correct her perspective. "And what do you mean, *want to embarrass you*?"

"You're always making sure everyone around knows when I mess up. You can never just speak to me. You need to make it a big deal," Sofia persists. "You literally looked around, to make sure everyone was watching."

Quickly taken aback by Sofia's allegations, she knew she needed to clarify the situation. "NO! I did no such thing, and I would not ever try to purposely embarrass you. I did look around, but it wasn't to *make sure everyone was watching*. It was so I could show you that everyone was scared for you too."

Sofia felt angered by her mother's talent at arguing, and she knew she couldn't prove that she was in the wrong, so she needed to expand further.

"Whatever. You even yelled at me in the store because some woman bumped into me, but you were upset that I didn't say excuse me," Sofia said confidently knowing her mother was in the wrong. She couldn't argue her way out of this one.

"No. You did in fact bump into that woman and you didn't have the decency to tell her you were sorry, or even excuse me," her mother insisted. "I didn't raise you to be so disrespectful. You have no idea what her life is like, or her day. A simple, I'm sorry or excuse me, could've made her day better. What if you made her feel unimportant?"

Sofia rolled her eyes in disbelief, her irritation growing stronger as her thoughts began to stir. Saying I'm sorry to someone does not make their day better, she thought. She has no idea how people work, but she just thinks she knows everything. Her thoughts continued to spiral as she glared through the window, wishing her mom would see things her way.

"Are you listening to me?" her mother asked interrupting her thoughts.

Infuriated by her mother's question, Sofia slung her head around facing her mother, and continued the argument.

"So now if I'm looking away, that means I'm not listening?" Sofia verbally shot back. "You stay on me about everything, even when I don't do anything wrong!"

"No, I don't," her mother replied. "If I correct you, it's not because I don't love you, it's because I do. You're young and things don't make sense, because when you're young you don't see the big picture. By correcting you I help you understand something that didn't make sense before, and correction makes you a better person as you grow older," she explained hoping it would make sense to her daughter.

"So constantly nit-picking me is supposed to make me be a better person?" Sofia asked dramatically, then began shaking her head.

"I don't nit-pick you," her mother insisted.

"Really? So, yelling at me for Isabella being annoying this morning, was supposed to *help* me. Oh, and the hour-long lectures I receive is supposed to *help* me?" Sofia petitioned urgently. "You just like making me feel like crap."

In disbelief her mother tried to open her daughters' eyes. "Your sister Isabella is only five years old. She loves you and adores you. She only asks you questions because you're her older sister and she will always find you fascinating. She takes everything you do and say to heart. Don't you want her to always have those feelings for you?" her mother replied. "I'd hate to see the two of you end up never speaking again. You never know what the future holds, and you should never speak to her that way."

"She's five. She's not going to remember anything. I'm fourteen and I don't remember anything from when I was five," Sofia persisted. "If she takes everything I say to heart, then when I told her that I didn't want to draw a picture with her, she should have listened. I have more important things to do."

Sofia began to feel frustrated that her mother was siding with her younger sister, and more importantly, she was flipping the entire situation. Something that mothers are good at.

She continued to listen with fury boiling in her gut, when her mother turned the conversation once more.

"There's going to be a time when she doesn't want to do things with you. Have you never thought about that?" her mother questioned. "You only refused because you were upset this morning, and you took out your frustration on her."

"I was upset because you were yelling at me all morning," Sofia argued with insistency. "Also, I wasn't taking my frustration out on her. We were leaving so there wasn't time. She wouldn't stop asking so it had to be said," Sofia ended her point with a swerve of her head.

"There was plenty of time. We didn't leave for another thirty minutes," her mother returned in a calm manner.

Sofia could feel the wall building up between the two, as though they had no connection at all. Her mother just didn't understand her, and she wasn't going to see it her way. This argument was going to last all day, and she was getting tired of it. If she wasn't going to listen, then there was no point in wasting her breath any longer.

"Forget it, you just love her more than me. You just think I'm so stupid, careless, and inconsiderate. It probably makes you feel better pointing it out so everyone else knows too," Sofia shot back.

"I can't believe you would say that. I am just trying to help you," said her mother as she reached for her arm.

Feeling her mother's touch, immediately made her feel sorry for her use of words, because her mother's touch always provides a calming sense of emotion. However, she didn't want to be calm, she wanted to be mad. This issue has gone on for so long, it needed to change. There was nothing that could make her anger or frustration go away. No amount of her mothers' explanations could help reason away how she constantly belittles her time and time again. She knew her mother didn't love her. She only said that to make herself feel better. She began to feel a sudden rise of emotion and she couldn't hold it in.

"Well, I don't want your help!" she shouted. "I don't need you. I wish you would leave me alone!"

After a slow release of breath in an effort to calm down, her mother attempts once more to reach Sofia. "Sofia, I know you're upset, but please don't stop talking to me. Please, let me in so I can help. Just talk to me."

Immediately feeling overwhelmed, Sofia just wants this conversation to end right now. In a rage filled outburst she yelled, "NO,

WILL YOU STOP! I DON'T WANT TO
TALK TO YOU EVER AGAIN!"

Her mother watched her daughter shout
those words in a fit of rage, as she turned back
to her solace gazing out the window. She must
have been so hurt inside to say such hurtful
words. There was nothing she could do but
shed a tear in silence. How she wished she still
had those days where all her daughter did was
want her nearby.

Her mother found the keys and placed
them in the ignition and just before she started
the car, she let out a sigh and said, "Here's a
good correction for you… one day you will
want to talk, but I won't be there."

After a long silent pause, the only
words spoken between the two were…

"Don't worry mother, I won't," Sofia
responded in a quiet sullen tone, still gazing out
the window.

It was then that her mother knew no
more words needed to be spoken. In this
moment they both just needed some silence.

She started up the car and began her
way back home painfully reliving the words her
daughter just spoke. How could she ever think
she didn't love her? Why does she see her love
in such a negative point of view. How will they
be able to get past this moment in time. She
could feel her heart pulling to her daughter as

she looked over at her wondering what could possibly be going through her mind.

Sofia instantly felt the regret of saying those things to her mother. She wanted to apologize, but her mother needed to know how strongly she felt about her wrongful criticisms. There was no other way. Once her mother realized that she was wrong, they can go back to normal, but for now she needed to get her point across. She's not a little girl anymore and her mother cannot step on her any longer because she is her own person. She remained silent, but deeply wanted to check on her mother, but her pride wouldn't allow her.

They sat in silence, as they drove through the parking lot, both longing for the need of one another. They made their way to the entrance to pull out onto the highway to return home when Sofia felt a sensation of remorse and compassionate pressure on her heart. Soon a power of will that compelled her to look at her mother just to see if she was okay overpowered her pride. She slowly turned her head, and her eyes caught her mother's as she saw the tears flowing out of her eyes. Her heart began to break to see her look so broken. Did her words really hurt her that badly? A simple glance at her mother turned into a lingering stare, and it wasn't long before her mother caught her glare. Sofia stared longingly into her mother's eyes as they turned the corner, and she noticed things she had never seen before. The wrinkles around her eyes, the lines across her forehead, and for a moment time felt as though it had slowed. What was mere seconds felt like an hour of her taking in her mother's face. How beautiful she was, but also how broken. As fast as time had slowed down, was as fast as time sped up and then in a blink of an eye…. her face was gone.

# *CHAPTER 2*

Sofia's mother's face had disappeared into a darkness, taken over by the lightening reflex reaction from the incident that shattered through their moment of reflection. Her eyes held tightly shut never allotting for a chance to sneak a peek into what she would forever remember as the symphonic melody of death.

Sofia remembered hearing a sound that began as a horn that multiplied in frequency like a foghorn that was being shoved into your ear. Her ears hadn't the chance to recover before the instant jolt of forceful impact was felt upon the right side of her back. Her body living out the discovery of Newton's law was met with an opposite reaction that was interrupted by the seatbelt securing her to her seat. She could feel each of her limbs being thrust about the cabin of the vehicle while feeling the different textures as they touched her. Her hand was slammed into the roof of the car, while her elbow met the car door. She could feel the hardness of the plastic paneling, and the soft cushion of the roof top. Her knees banging into the hard dashboard, and her head being slung into the window. There were loud sounds of breaking glass, screeching metal, thuds, booms, snapping. The right hemisphere of her head grazed something quite coarse, that felt as though a dull razor was peeling off her skin. She could feel small cuts appearing on her arms and face, like a thousand paper cuts all happening in unison. Her neck snapping each time it was whipped around from one side to the other, front ways and back. The only part of her that felt immobile was her torso, as it was still held tightly in place. The smell infused her nostrils with an aroma of burning metal, like what one smells when they weld. An oil scent mixed with a smoky hint could be inhaled with each pound into the road. Her senses were heightened to experience what she could not see, as the whirlwind of the crash instinctively caused her eyes to remain shut. However, she could see the dance of their wreck perfectly in her mind. They were spinning in the air, perfectly in time with the scraps of metal that were breaking off and joining them midair in perfect synchronization. Then the loud boom of their car slamming down on the pavement, as the dwindling sound of metal squishing together, glass falling to the ground, slowly ending with a soft whisper of the gusts of air around them.

All traffic around them had ceased as the audience near witnessed a single car tossed into the air by the shear collision of a semi-truck meeting the back end of their small car. The emotional turmoil felt by each person entering or leaving the mall could be felt by all. The semi had apparently tried to miss them but wound up nailing their back end and turning his rig on its side, skidding into the ditch.

As seconds past, there remained silence, as one person looked to the other to see what lie beneath the wreckage. The dust from impact still filled the air but all horrific evidence could be seen. A mangled car turned over, that couldn't be identified when looking at the back side of it. Glass and metal pieces scattered about between the two vehicles. The semi in the ditch endured minimal damage but was still engulfed in a dust storm from skidding into the dirt-filled ditch. It was the longest wave of silence that ever existed at that intersection. For a moment all that could be heard were the whistling sounds of air escaping the engine of the two vehicles. When soon a loud creak echoed across the crowd. Through the cloud of dust, a silhouette could be seen. It was the driver of the semi who seemed to make his way out of the truck in a confused state. He appeared holding his head, with an anguishing look upon his face. The moment he was seen, a single voice was heard over the audience…

"SOMEONE CALL 9-1-1!" a bystander called out, and soon the silence was no more. Several people rushed to the truck driver's side, reassuring him he would be okay. Others rushed to check on Sofia and her mom, but the lack of movement left people afraid. There soon were roadblocks created to keep people back, and before you knew it, the dreadful sound of sirens could be deciphered through the crowd. Their screeching noise grew louder and louder until the sound perforated the unconscious mind of Sofia.

Steps could be heard growing louder and sounded fast paced. While she wasn't completely conscious, she was able to make out some sounds. Soon someone had reached her side of the car.

"ARE YOU OKAY?" a strange man called out. "CAN YOU HEAR ME?" he shouted again, desperately trying to get even the simplest response from Sofia. Just looking at her lifeless body could scare anyone and worry that this accident would be one where some didn't walk away.

With the sound of his voice reverberating off the walls of her mind, she began to awaken through the fogginess that clouded her brain. The strange man's voice continued to echo in her head as he continued to reassure her. His voice began to hurt her head, and she switched her attention to the fact that her rag doll body lied on a hot surface that felt like it was made with nails. She felt as though her chest was drenched in water, perhaps something spilled, but she couldn't recall bringing a drink into the car with her. Her seatbelt must have given way eventually because she was no longer secure, although she hadn't been launched out the window, so it obviously did its job. Every miniscule movement was made in pain. Every breath was regretted. She could hear people's feet shuffling through broken glass as they made their way closer, but her vision appeared impaired, as she was unable to make out clearly the images in front of her. But the ting, ting, ting of each shard of glass was a sound that was clear as day.

"DON'T MOVE! THE PARAMEDICS ARE ON THEIR WAY!" the man assured her.

A few seconds later, paramedics made their way to their car. Before she could gather the courage to breathe enough air to speak, she felt the coldness of a man's hand in hers. Then a gentle voice followed through, "Hello, my name is Peter, I am a paramedic, and everything is going to be okay. You've been in an accident, and we are going to safely remove you from the vehicle and get you to the hospital."

Sofia's mind began to race. Accident? What's going on? She thought unable to speak her concerns out loud. Soon she could hear another person's voice near her, and she listened to them talk while they followed procedure to check her. While they did, she longed to ask the only question that came to mind. She couldn't remember seeing or hearing her mother and her heart ached for an answer. She breathed in deeply and asked, "Where's…… my m---" and then it all went dark. Sofia had passed out.

Suddenly, she could feel something painful but couldn't locate in her mind where it was. She then felt them move her onto the gurney. This time, the pain was felt all over, their touch on her neck, arms, and side was aching. The movement of her limbs as she was drug out of the wreckage and placed onto the gurney was excruciating; so much that the pain felt overwhelming. She felt each piece of glass dig into her as her body slid across the shards. Struggling to keep herself conscious, she looked to the man who called himself Peter. Reaching in painful agony she was able to grab his hand and ask once more, "Where's my mom?"

Those words flowing from her mouth gave her a sense of accomplishment, because she was unable to ask the full question before. She blinked and released the air she built up and waited.

He looked to the other paramedic with fear in his eyes. After sharing their unspoken thoughts his look returned in a soft reassuring expression and he said, "Your mother is being transported as well. Please, don't worry. We need you to stay calm."

With those last words that Peter said, she had received reassurance that her mother too had survived, and all would be okay. The pain radiated throughout her body, and she couldn't bear to lie awake any longer, and into the darkness she crept again.

Sofia is in and out of consciousness as she is rushed to the emergency room, but her mother is not there with her. She reassures herself that her mom is in another ambulance, on her way, and she will see her there. She can't help but wonder if she was truly okay.

The people surrounding her seem to be weary of what is going on. They are shouting to each other, calling out information that she doesn't quite understand. They are making notes, and constantly feeling her wrist. It's chaos, but the worst part was not that she didn't understand what they were talking about. It's the fear she could see in their every movement, but what were they afraid of? Her endless confusion puts her back into her slumber until all at once a halting shriek shakes the entire ambulance as it comes to an abrupt stop.

The doors burst open and there's even more voices heard all around her. She is awakened by the banging of the wheels of the gurney rolling off the ambulance and smashing into the ground. She's feeling a jolt of energy and begins to look around. There's another ambulance in the distance but no one is near it or coming out of it. It's just sitting there. Immediately she panics and looks for her mother, but her mother is nowhere to be found. Nervousness creeps in and she gets scared even more. She thinks to herself that they may have lied to her to spare her the truth. She needs them to tell her the truth. "WHERE IS MY MOM? IS SHE OKAY? I WANT MY MOM!", Sofia yells frantically as she yanks off her oxygen mask.

The nurses on each side rest their hands on her shoulders and then the one on the left began to plea with her as she grabs her mask from her simultaneously. "PLEASE. Calm down honey, your mom is going to be okay. She's already been admitted into the hospital, and we're going to do everything we can so you can see her soon."

"NO, I WANT MY MOM! LET ME SEE HER, NOW!" she yelled back once more. Feeling as though that was all she had to give.

"Please be still sweetie," the nurse calmly tells her as she looks directly into her eyes. "You are very hurt. I promised your mom when she came in, I would do whatever I need to do to save your life. Don't make me break my promise to your mother." You could see the dedication to her word in her eyes, as she made very clear what Sofia needed to do.

Her heart began to race, faster and faster. As she laid calmly on the gurney being rushed around the hospital she realized, her mother was alive. She needed her to do what they said. Her heartbeat and the rhythm of the lights that passed her eyes began to sync. She had no idea where they were taking her, or where her mother could be. Was she okay? Was she hurt too? Her questions were left unanswered. Tears flowed from her eyes dripping down the sides of her face. She hurt so much, but the worry she had for her mother hurt more.

Then in a quickness, a rising power of pain had overtaken Sofia in that moment, and she began to lose the ability to breathe. There are not many times in a person's life, that they consider if this shall be the time of their death, but for Sofia, that time was right now. She closed her eyes in agonizing pain, feeling her lungs desperately desiring air, until she realized she wasn't as strong as she once thought. The pain grew more and more as they made their way down the hall. The more immense the pain grew, the less she could see, feel, or hear. In the climax of the torture all the light in the nurses' faces were soon gone. Then the room was dimmed, and all that was left was the sound of her heartbeat and the rhythmic flashes of lights above her. Finally, the inevitability of darkness won once more.

# *CHAPTER 3*

Stirring in her slumber Sofia feels a warm and cozy sensation. All the pain she had once felt was no longer overpowering her, only peacefulness filled her every sense. Did they heal her? Is she all better? These questions helped entice her to awaken, as she desperately needed to know what happened to her mother and if she was okay. Or maybe it was all a horrible dream.

She opened her eyes slowly to escape the nightmare she had, only to realize that the darkness was still there. How could a dark place be so warm and yet scary? She sat upright, but no one was around. She was all alone. She sat there baffled by this confusing place, wondering where she was, and what was she doing there? It was empty, all around an endless darkness. You couldn't tell the difference between the walls, ceiling, or floor. Everywhere you turned was pitch black.

Starting to frighten, she began to call out to the only person she knew could make her feel safe, "MOM?" she called out, but not a sound was heard. The feeling of her chest began to weigh her down, and her breaths started to sound heavy. The void around her started closing in, until she felt she couldn't breathe. Her eyes began to water, and she slowly curled herself into a ball disheartened by her loneliness and then….

In the distance she could see a small spec that closely resembled a spec of glitter. Sofia, swayed from side to side seeing if it moved at all. Once she realized that she wasn't envisioning it, she could feel an urge to go toward it. Slowly she picked herself up and took a few steps with great hesitation between each stride. The closer she got, the bigger it grew, and soon she realized that it wasn't a spec…. it was LIGHT! THERE WAS LIGHT!

Immediately she sprinted for the way out. The closer she got, the more joy she felt. The warmth she was feeling was coming from there. That's where the peacefulness is, and that's where she wanted to be. Each breath of air she took was like taking a breath of hope. A single whiff alone could fill your soul with optimism for days. She knew that within the light, held all her answers. Her mother would be there, and they would be together again. Sofia couldn't wait to see her mother and figure out what happened to them. Just as she went to enter the light and leave the darkness, she was covered in serenity. All emotion of terror, worry, fret, had vanished, and she knew she needed to be in the light. One step into the white room and Sofia was overtaken with an emotion so fulfilling, she knew that it couldn't be mistaken for anything else. She felt love. A love so deep and pure, only when one closes their eyes and shuts everything else out, can they absorb the depths of love being thrust upon them. She simply took it in.

She lost track of thought, and forgot where she was, what had happened, and all past anger she had held. In the midst of her captivation, she felt a sudden tap, tap, tap on her shoulder and a voice that called out to her.

Sofia jumped with a fright because she had every indication that she was alone. The shrieking vocals she had let loose could have shattered glass, thankfully there was none around.

Sofia had spun around to find out who was there, but it wasn't who she would have ever expected. The first glance was a bright light that radiated in your eyes. It glowed luminously, but the longer you stared the dimmer the light appeared. As the light disappeared Sofia was able to identify what was in front of her.

The light had turned into a woman, a woman she didn't know. She was dressed all in white, with bright red hair. She had a glow about her that welcomed your soul into hers and enraptured your every thought. Sofia was enthralled by her, that she couldn't focus on anything the woman had said, and she had a lot to say.

"I'M SO SORRY!" the lady blurted out apologetically. "I didn't mean to scare you; I am always doing that! I've really got to work on that, but you know, how are you supposed to know when to introduce yourself. I mean people stand there and they will stand forever, you know. Is it one minute, five, ten? I mean ten is probably too long, to just be awkwardly standing around someone lingering at them. Wouldn't that make me a stalker, although I am not hanging out in the trees or anything like that, so I guess not."

Sofia, was in shock, not only did some stranger just tap her on the shoulder when no one else was around, but she was rambling on talking a hundred miles an hour making the situation even more weird. She took a second as the lady continued to talk about stalkers, and she finally found the words.

"Wait a minute, who are you and where did you come from?" Sofia asked interrupting her meaningless speech.

"Oh, my goodness, where are my manners? My name is Angelica, it's very nice to meet you, I am so sorry I frightened you, I didn't mean to. I know you were enjoying all the feelings and the warmth. I mean it's amazing, but we do have to get a move on. There's just so much to discuss, because there's the crash, your death, and where you end up… oh dear this could take forever…. But I mean we do have eternity, right?" Angelica says as she chuckles by her own amusement.

"DEATH!" Sofia interrupts Angelica's laughter. "WHAT DO YOU MEAN DEATH?" Sofia was shocked about what she had heard. *DIE.* How could she be dead? She wasn't dead, there was no way. She looked to the lady in shocking dismay and waited for her to correct her obvious mistake.

"Oh, I'm sorry, did I say death? No, that's incorrect, although you are dying. I don't know if that helps but if you really think about it, I'm sure it helps in a small way," Angelica stated attempting to correct her mistake.

"I-I-don't understand," Sofia said softly. "How could I die? This can't be happening." She stood in contemplation trying to figure out how things could've possibly turned out like this, when a high-pitched voice chimed in once more.

"It's happening. Hmm…. I wonder if I should've given you more time before I said that. Maybe a few seconds more for you to grasp the concept? Hmm... Oh well, moving on," Angelica said as she started walking away quite vivaciously.

Sofia started to feel annoyed that this woman was taking her *death* with such whimsy. How could she just drop a bomb on someone like that, and frolic away as if she just won a free ice cream? This type of information cannot just be given with a smile, and everyone just be perfectly fine with it. NO! That woman was going to tell her what was going on, and she was going to do it right now. Sofia turned around ready to demand answers, when she realized she was no longer in a room of light. She was somewhere she had never seen before, although she could feel as if she had been there at one point in time. She was connected to the place in her heart.

The illumination of scenery was captivating and was nothing ever seen on any corner of the earth. Just before her was a giant golden gate that stretched far into the sky. In the middle there was a tree emblem resembled the tree of life. As Sofia walked closer, she could see that just beyond that was a place filled with gold streets, that sparkled and shined a gold hue. There were mansions as far as the eye could see. There even appeared to be castles on top of one another separated by luminous gold clouds, as if each part of the sky were different streets. There was joyous music that filled the air in a romantic kind of way. Harps, violins, cellos, pianos, the sound of a classical orchestra was the only way to interpret the whimsy sound. It was beautiful to the eyes, and sweet to the heart. Soft praises could be heard in the distance, and she forgot about everything for a moment. She couldn't help but feel pure happiness, and love. The most beautiful painting or photograph would never be able to capture what she was seeing. Then, a loud snap woke her from her trance. Angelica had snapped her fingers in front of her face to get her back on track.

"Hello!" Angelica said flitting her hand in front of Sofia's face to get her attention. "I know it's AMAZING! Believe me, it's even better if you actually get to stay here, and there's a good chance that you won't. So, if you would follow me, we can begin with everything that we need to discuss starting with your horrible attitude towards everyone around you. They seem to always be hit with hatefulness when you're around. Even your poor sister, and mother… wow. You're always taking your anger out on those who love you. Well strangers too, but I can tell you don't take them into consideration, am I right?"

Angelica nudges Sofia as if she had just made a joke, but Sofia cannot help but feel offended by each sentence that comes out of her mouth. She gets furious with her accusations because she doesn't know her. She doesn't know anything about her.

"WHO DO YOU THINK YOU ARE?" Sofia yelled. "You don't know anything about me. I don't know you, and you don't know me. You have no idea who I get mad at or if I treat people badly. Which I do not. So, why don't you mind your business."
Sofia felt she had made her point, and that Angelica would cease the conversation. Unfortunately for Sofia, Angelica was unaffected.

"You're darling," Angelica said with a smile and proceeded to walk around her. With Sofia's gaze on her, the beauty of the golden city that once surrounded her slowly faded away.

Confused, Sofia waited for Angelica to start her rambling as it appeared she did quite often.

"I do in fact know you. You're fourteen, you used to shove food around in the house so you wouldn't have to eat it when you were five. You tripped your best friend because you were mad at her and told everyone that Jessica your other friend had done it. You get bad grades and blame it on the teachers. You curse when you think no one will find out, and you bite your nails on a regular basis. Also, on the day of your accident you had a fight with your mother, hurt your sisters' feelings, and even treated a stranger disrespectfully in the mall, due to your frustration you had towards your mother," Angelica said quickly.

"How did you know that?" Sofia asked.

"Because I know you my dear. I've watched you your whole life. I mean I don't watch you all the time, I mean that would be weird. I have other people I keep tabs on, not that you needed to know that. Although I am sure it helps, so you know that I'm not some crazy person you see on those late-night televisions shows. But maybe my comparison of the two highlights the similarities more… hmm. I should work on that too," Angelica said as she eventually trailed off on some sort of tangent that got difficult to make out as she spoke softer and softer.

"Wait, I am confused," Sofia said alarmingly. "You've been watching me? You know me? I'm dying?"

She couldn't help feeling overwhelmed and suddenly released a loud angry shout, "I just don't unders--- UGH! CAN SOMEONE, OTHER THAN THIS RAMBLING IDOT, TELL ME WHAT IS HAPPENING?" Sofia began to scream into the abyss as if maybe someone else could possibly hear her plea and appear out of nowhere just as Angelica had previously. She let out a gust of breath to release her rising anxiety, but she only felt worse.

She began to get scared again, fearful of what was happening and the fact that she couldn't make sense of anything. Sofia dropped to her knees and let out a plea to whoever could hear her. "Where's my mom? I want to see my mother!" she cried softly.

Angelica could sense that this introduction had not gone as planned. She needed to change direction if they were ever going to get back on track. She softly rested her hand on Sofia's shoulder, and she said, "Let me release you of your worries my dear, so you can understand better."

Through each second her feelings began to fade and turn into a calmer and understanding emotion. Her mind began to clear, and she sensed she was ready to listen.

Angelica took a moment and gathered herself and her thoughts. She took a deep breath and said, "I'm sorry Sofia. Sometimes I get overwhelmed by all the information of a person that I cannot help but to let it all out at once. I want so badly to help you, that I want to jump in and get started. I forget that people need a chance to process little by little, because their minds and their hearts are not in tune with one another. So, let's take this one step at a time to help you understand. Okay?"

Sofia felt better knowing that this situation was finally going to make sense and she agreed to hear her out.

"Where would you like to start?" Angelica asks her.

"Who are you?" Sofia asked after thinking for a second.

Baffled by the simplicity of her question she replied, "I am Angelica, my dear," and she let out a chuckle. "You don't grasp the obvious stuff do you, huh love. We might have to take this slower than I thought."

"No. I mean, who are you to me. I've never seen you before in my life. You also have a way of completely changing my emotions like some sort of superpower. Also, no one I have ever met glows the way you do," Sofia stated clarifying Angelica's take on her question.

"OH! Right, I'm sorry. Went way over my head there. Can you say Dunce table for one." Angelica said laughing at her own mistakes.

"So... *Who*, or *what* are you?" Sofia asked once more slightly annoyed.

"I'm an Angel my dear," Angelica said. "And what you have seen is a little taste of Heaven."

# *Chapter 4*

Heaven. How could this be? I mean, Wow! Heaven. Heaven is what I just saw! I've seen it with my very own eyes, that's amazing, Sofia, thought to herself in utter amazement. Heaven is not only real, but it's a place that mere words would not ever be able to explain. While her thoughts slowly absorbed the information she had been given, her heart and her mind began to align. She was ready to hear Angelica out, and to understand what had happened to her.

"Okay, so you're an angel, and have been watching me my whole life. Would that make you my guardian angel?" Sofia asked.

"Yes. You get it! Great, now we can move on," Angelica said excitedly as she began to walk away.

"Wait, wait, wait," Sofia called to her jumping to her feet. "If you've been with me my whole life, then why can I see you now, if I'm not completely dead."

"Because humans are selfish, and the thing about selfishness is that it only allows you to see what you desire," Angelica explains as she continues to walk away. "This creates a blindness. Even though people can make selfless acts, it's not enough until their hearts are completely clean for them to rid themselves of the blindness, they have caused themselves."

Not fully understanding what Angelica means, Sofia decides to move on to another question that is festering inside her.

"Okay, then answer me this, if you're my guardian angel, then why weren't you guarding me? Isn't that like you're job?"

Abruptly, Angelica stopped in her tracks. She turns and tilts her head, her eyes meeting Sofia's out the corner of her eyes. She smiles asking her one simple question, "So you think it's my fault that you're dying."

"Umm, well kind of," Sofia says dramatically.

Angelica swiftly comes back to her, as if she had flown. The next thing she knew they were both sitting comfortably in the softest white chairs. They were so soft anyone could fall asleep in them. Between them appeared a table with dainty floral china and a tea pot.

Angelica began to pour them some tea as she explained herself.

"My dear, let me explain how this works. Guardian angels cannot keep you out of trouble although it would save a lot of time. We simply speak to your heart to help you understand the situations *you* get yourself into, and boy you humans can get yourselves into some pickles. One lump or two?" Angelica asks while she holds a cube of sugar in front of her.

Sofia, nods to Angelica signaling for two cubes as she continues to listen.

"You see, there are moments where you are doing something, talking, or just in the midst of making a decision, and you feel a pressing feeling in your heart. That is us," Angelica explains as she stirs her tea. "God gave you the gift of free will, which means we cannot control you. We are there to guide you through life. For instance, do you remember a pressing feeling to check on your mother after your argument, just to make sure she was okay?"

Angelica glanced at her waiting for Sofia to remember then began explaining again.

"When I placed my hand on your shoulder earlier and you felt calm and a desire to understand. That is how it works. We speak into your heart because that's where God is. It's where all your understanding, compassion,

patience, mercy, and love is found.
Unfortunately, people don't always listen, and
decide to make the wrong choices anyway. It's
because your mind is telling you to do one
thing, and your heart is telling you to do
another."

Angelica pauses for a moment to make
sure Sofia is understanding. She waits patiently
sipping her tea.

"We cannot keep bad things from
happening. Those bad things are a result from
your own broken world," Angelica explains.

"So, my dying is my fault?" Sofia
slowly expresses.

"No, my dear. You humans are always
trying to point the finger," Angelica states a
little exasperated. "This is no one's fault.
However, the best lessons learned are through
tribulation, and sometimes through our
mistakes we can help others too."

"So, this is a lesson?" Sofia asks.

"Yes!" Angelica replies placing her
finger on her nose.

"What lesson do I need to learn?" Sofia
asked disdainfully.

"Perfect question. Now we can move
on!" Angelica said jumping to her feet quite
vivaciously as the chairs and tea disappeared.
However, Sofia was caught off guard and she
fell straight to her bottom. Leaping up

dramatically, she chased after Angelica to hear what she had to say.

"You see love, I was sent to you by God to save you, to help you learn. Unfortunately, you have not made the best choices in your life, and therefore you either need to learn from your mistakes or face the consequences," Angelica said.

"What consequences? What mistakes?" Sofia asks as she tries to keep up with the pace of Angelica.

"Well fourteen years is a lot of mistakes to cover, so let's just focus on the mistakes leading up to your accident," Angelica says. "First you…"

"Wait accident?" Sofia interrupted because she somehow had forgotten the whole reason she was there.

"Yes, you and your mother were in a car accident as you left the mall. It was a dreadful sight." Angelica exclaimed showing signs of sadness, as she continued to describe the horrific scene.

As Sofia listened her mind flashed of every bit of detail from the crash. Pictures fleeting through her mind as if they were on a slideshow. She could recall it all. She couldn't believe she had forgotten.

All this information of guardian angels and heaven made her completely forget about what event brought her here in the first place.

Collecting each piece of information in her mind, she remembered the most important question that needed to be asked.

"Wait, I'm dying. Where's my mom? Did she live? I thought she was alive. Is she okay?" Sofia asked as quickly as the words could leave her mouth.

"Your mother is exactly where she needs to be, and she is safe," Angelica reassures her as she places her hands on her arms. "You need to be more concerned about if you will be. I mean if that even worries you at all."

Sofia took a second to analyze what Angelica just said. *Worries me at all*. Sofia thought. What's that's supposed to mean? She was glad to know her mother was safe, but she couldn't help but wonder what she had meant by that comment. Of course, she was concerned about her situation, why wouldn't she be. Then she realized that the situation might be worse than she thought.

"I am concerned," Sofia insisted. "So…. what mistakes, and what consequences?" She asked again, to get back on track now that she knew her mother was okay.

"On the day of the accident you were horrible. There was no love, compassion, kindness, or anything in your heart that day. I couldn't get through to you at all," Angelica said. "You were mean to your younger sister. Careless towards a stranger. Then you were downright hateful to your own mother. Who, by the way, is incredibly patient with you. You should probably thank Jeffrey for that."

"Who's Jeffrey?" Sofia asked confused.

"Your mother's guardian angel, but don't worry it will just confuse you even more. I probably shouldn't have brought him up. Anyways, let's get to the consequences," Angelica responded.

Sofia took in a deep breath bracing herself for what she was about to hear. If there were anyway, she could have prepared herself, she would have done it ten times over.

"The consequences my dear is an eternity in hell," Angelica said just as easily as asking for a piece of pie.

"I'M GOING TO HELL!" Sofia shouted as she started to panic.

"Maybe, yes," Angelica said.

Sofia was starting to get upset over Angelica's easy-going manner. She was not very good at this. How can she just blurt these things out all willy-nilly. "What do you mean, *maybe*?" Sofia asked frustratingly.

"Well, you have three lessons to learn," Angelica replied. "God has this thing for the number three. I don't know if you've ever caught on to that, but I find it quite wonderful."

"ANYWAYS…," Sofia interrupted to get Angelica back on track

"Anyways, if you're able to learn from these lessons, you will spend eternity in Heaven. However, if you should not, then you must live with the pain that you have caused all for all of eternity," Angelica said spelling it out for her.

"ARE YOU KIDDING ME!" shouted Sofia. "You're telling me that one bad day, is going to cost me Heaven? How is that even fair?"

Anger didn't begin to describe how Sofia was feeling. She had always been told about Heaven. How if we believe we will get to go there when we die. But now, all of a sudden if we even have a difficult day, we are denied. Her thoughts filled with anguish. What fine print did she forget to read?

Angelica intervened to explain, "It's not a bad day that gets you denied. It's the decisions you make throughout your life. It's the actions you make in your life that all lead up to your death on which the decision is made."

"I just don't understand, I go to church. I volunteer sometimes. I do good things. Those are good actions," Sofia argued.

"It's not about the deeds that we do. Good deeds don't tell a person's heart, their intentions behind their actions do," Angelica explained. "For example, a man can donate to charity, but only do it so he can claim it on his taxes. A woman can have a high-ranking position in a church, but gossip about everyone in the congregation. A child can volunteer, but only because their parents forced them to. Good deeds are great, but they don't define a person, their heart does. Just because your body fills the pew, doesn't mean your heart belongs to Jesus."

Sofia thought about her heart that day, and Angelica was right. There wasn't any love in her heart that day, but she still couldn't understand how the arguments that she was speaking of could possibly cause her to be in trouble. Afterall, it was everyone else's fault, she did nothing wrong.

"Then why isn't everyone else punished?" Sofia asked. "They are the reason I had a bad day. They made me feel that way. What punishment are they going to get?"

Angelica's expression changed from joy to sadness, and with a forced smile and a disheartened look, she looked into her eyes and said, "They've already been punished my dear."

Confused, Sofia asked, "By who?"

"You," Angelica replied.

"ME? I haven't done anything to them," Sofia stated wondering how she could've been their punisher.

Angelica appeared disheartened and then she closed her eyes like she was listening to something in the distance. When she opened her eyes, she looked as if she knew something that Sofia did not. Sofia was intrigued to know what it was. Angelica began to glow a fierce light that shined deep into your soul. Her feet rose off the ground, her eyes glowed, and she spoke in a stringent voice.

"I can tell you truly feel as though you have done nothing wrong," Angelica expressed in a haunting tone. "However, that does not make it true. For this, you must learn your lessons. I promise you it will be hard. If you are unwilling to accept the challenge that lies before you, then your fate has already been sealed."

Sofia was scared unexpectedly. Angelica was so sweet and innocent, that she never expected to ever fear her. Her tone was not her own, and it felt as though she were being scolded by a superior being. She was afraid, because the fate she spoke of, was eternal damnation. She gazed at her as she floated luminously and realized that she could either accept it or change it. The thought of three lessons seemed to be simple enough, but Angelica had promised they would be hard, but how? The fate of her eternity lied within a simple answer, and as she thought she remembered her mother and what she would want her to do. She gathered up her strength and with a look of determination, she answered Angelica, "Let's change my fate."

# *Chapter 5*

After agreeing to Angelica's terms, Sofia worried, what if she wouldn't be able to learn the lessons? She contemplated the outcome but decided that there was nothing to fret about. She decided that the outcome would remain the same, because it would not be what Angelica expected. She would see the truth, and the truth was that she was not the one at fault. It was everyone else. It was them who caused her to get upset. It was their fault because they didn't understand her or what she had been going through or feeling. They were the ones who were not compassionate. The outcome was obvious, it wasn't for her to change it was for them, and soon it would be evident.

"So how does this work? Are we just going to sit around a television and watch what happened?" asked Sofia now suddenly optimistic about the challenge.

"Umm…. No," Angelica replied with a slight chuckle. "You're so cute. No, we are going to encounter. It's really a lot of fun. My first time was amazing, it really tickled in my stomach, although I was so scared, I threw up," Angelica started laughing at the fond memories she held. Although, Sofia found her memories quite disturbing and gross for that matter.

"Uh, yea. Sounds amazing," Sofia said sarcastically. "So, what does encounter mean?"

"My dear girl, have you never opened a dictionary? No wonder you don't make very good grades, even your books are scared to be around you," Angelica jokingly stated.

However, Sofia wasn't as amused as her guardian angel. Some guardian angel she is, she can't even guard her feelings, Sofia thought.

Angelica could tell that Sofia didn't like her joke at all as she appeared to be sour about her comment. She thought for a moment trying to find the best way to explain her behavior to Sofia. Then she knew exactly what to say.

"I'm sorry Sofia, I was just kidding. You're usually a very sarcastic person, so I figured that it was the best way to get connected with you, and make you feel comfortable. But if it makes you upset then I would rather not speak that way. Okay?" Angelica apologized.

Understanding that Angelica was just trying to help her feel comfortable, and that she didn't mean those things in a negative way. Sofia decided that maybe it would be okay to allow her an inch in.

"It's okay. I'm sure you only thought it was funny because the only sense of humor you have is a dead one," Sofia replied looking at her out the corner of her eye with a slight smirk signaling sarcasm.

Angelica instinctively sensed the comical tone in Sofia's voice and caught her glance. With a huge smile she began to nod in agreement with her play on words. She couldn't help but join in with the banter that had been created between the two of them.

"That was a real *dead* joke there," Angelica said and proceeded to laugh hysterically. "Oh, my goodness, that was delightful. I haven't heard a joke that caught me off guard like that since Lucille Ball."

"Lucille Ball?" Sofia questioned. "Of all the comedians out there, that's who you reference?"

"Of course, my dear, us red heads need to stick together," Angelica said winking at Sofia.

Shaking her head at Angelica, Sofia decided to change the subject. "So, can you tell me what encountering is or not?" She asked this time hoping for an actual answer, but with

Angelica, she knew there was a possibility that would not happen.

Angelica could sense that now was the time to explain. While she enjoyed their growing connection, it was time to get a move on, if they were ever going to change her fate.

"Encounter. To unexpectedly experience or meet someone unexpectedly," Angelica responded with a grin.

Sofia was frustrated because even with an actual answer, she still had no idea what that meant. Frankly made her feel quite stupid. Maybe she did scare her books away. Nonetheless, she needed to know what it meant, maybe through a more simplistic idea. So, she decided to break it down.

"So, I'm going to meet someone unexpectedly?" Sofia asked.

"No," Angelica stated quickly.

"Huh?" confused Sofia responded.

"You will not physically meet them; however, you will experience things unexpectedly, and you will face people unexpectedly," Angelica explained.

Angelica's explanation was simple, but it was also filled with mystery. Meeting someone without meeting them, and facing them, without knowing them? That was the vaguest understanding that had ever brought meaning to something that Sofia had ever heard.

"Okay, so we are randomly going around seeing people without meeting them," Sofia said out loud trying to make sense of it all.

"Yes!" said Angelica.

"So, we're going to stalk people?" Sofia interjected poking fun at Angelica who had previously went on a tangent regarding the topic.

"I AM NOT A STALKER! That's not it at all. You really turned that right around didn't you. I bet your teachers *love* explaining things to you," Angelica replied obviously offended and slowly going off on another one of her tangents. Unfortunately, this one was taking a turn, and she wasn't making a lot of sense.

"I bet when someone tells you it is raining cats and dogs you look to the sheer blue skies trying to catch a new pet. Or if someone says there's a walking encyclopedia you start looking down the road, or if..."

Sofia knew that all signs pointed to the fact that she most likely would not stop talking. Therefore, Sofia interrupted Angelica as she realized that her small comment quickly erupted her into a whirlwind of verbal rant.

"I'm sorry. It was a joke. You know ha, ha. My goodness, we just had a conversation about trying to find our connection. I was only trying to connect with you," Sofia said releasing a breath of air and rolling her eyes wishing she had never made the comment in the first place. With a huff she asked, "So how does encountering work?"

After taking a moment to gather herself Angelica returned to her normal bubbly self which took mere seconds. "Well basically I will wrap you in my wings and carry you to our destination," Angelica stated once again in her bubbly tone gliding her hand through the air.

"Wings? You don't have wings," Sofia corrected by stating the obvious. For Angelica stood before her, without a feather in sight.

"Oh, my dear, wings like you wouldn't believe," Angelica said with her eyes lighting up.

She breathed in deeply and out appeared the most beautiful pair of wings that protruded from her shoulder bones. They appeared so rapidly that Sofia jumped back from shock. They were magnificent, radiant, and shined a gold hue around them. They shimmered in dancing sparkles. Each feather had a metallic pearl white color, that as the light hit them you could see each dazzling spec of glitter. They appeared soft to the touch, and indeed they were, as Sofia found out when she reached to touch them. Their romantic look engulfed her thoughts and for a moment all she could think about was what it must feel like to be wrapped up in them.

"They are gorgeous," Sofia said quietly in astonishment.

"I know!" Angelica said in an elevated manner, and she tucked her wings away as they were before.

"Why don't you always have them out?" Sofia asked.

"Because it's very hard for people to stay focused when they are out. I mean come on. How often do you get to see something like that?" Angelica stated. "So, are you ready to learn the first lesson?"

Acknowledging Angelica's reasoning, Sofia wondered what exactly the lessons are she needs to learn. How will she know if she's learned them? She quickly asked to soothe her questioning mind, "Okay, but first what are the lessons I need to learn?"

"Oh, I cannot tell you that my dear. If I told you then you wouldn't learn them," she replied. "I mean, if you were to take a test and someone gave you all the answers, would you have learned anything?"

"But if I don't know what to study for, then how am I going to find the answers?" Sofia returned with a rebuttal.

Angelica sees how Sofia was understanding this situation, and felt she needed to explain just a little more.

"My dear, I cannot tell you anything about where we will go, what you will see, or what you should learn. What you learn will show your heart. You cannot fake it. You cannot change it. It is what it is. No matter which way a person goes their heart will always tell the truth."

The uncertainty that was approaching Sofia felt heavy because she had no idea what to expect. Her heart, Angelica said, no one else's. That means, they would not be paying attention to everyone else, only to her. The realization nearly paralyzed her, because now she understood that the outcome was not certain. With rising worry, she questioned in thought, what if she learned a lesson, but it was the wrong one? Everything was going to be riding on this, and she was unsure in this moment if her fate would change at all.

"So, then what do I do? How am I supposed to learn?" Sofia asked nervously.

"You watch and listen. The answers will find you soon enough, or they won't," Angelica responded with a shrug of her shoulders and perky tone at the end of her sentence. Then she reached out her hand and waited for Sofia.

There was no other option. No other details. There was only the one chance in front of her, and even though she was unsure, there wasn't anything else she could do. With hesitation she thought of the nurse who walked beside her rushing her into the hospital. Her words lingered in her mind.

*Don't let me break my promise to your mother.* Her mother wanted her life to be saved. Even though, she would not live to see another day, she knew this life is just as important.

Sofia knew that her mother would be in Heaven one day, and if she would ever be with her again, she would need to save her own life. Her eternal life that is.

Nervously enough, Sofia looked to the hand held out to her realizing the opportunity in front of her and took Angelica's hand in hers. Angelica could feel her worries, and as her wings slowly wrapped around her. She looked to Sofia and said, "I must warn you, some of what you see may be difficult to bear, but do not be afraid, I am here, and you will be fine."

Her words were meant to comfort her, but all they managed to do was frighten her. Sofia's body began to tremble, and her nerves were taking over. With her terror increasing, everything around her started to change, and there was no turning back now.

Thousands of light streams shined from them, and her body began to tingle. The streams of light turned golden, and they began to widen. They soon fused together getting brighter and brighter. Until everything around her turned white and for a moment she was experiencing blindness. The only thing she could make out was the feeling of her body, which felt as though she was on a roller coaster she couldn't escape from. As the bright light began to fade the images around her were made clear. Suddenly, her feet could feel solid ground. Her body began to ache, and the tingling sensation was gone. However, the disappearance of the tingling was replaced with a surprising new sensation that appeared in her stomach. Sadly, it was a queasy feeling. Then all at once Angelica released her of her wings and Sofia gazed around, but where was she? She had never been here before. As her curiosity rose, so did her bodily fluids and with that Angelica was able to reminisce over her first time.

With joy in her heart Angelica looked at Sofia who was hung over at the waist, releasing horrific sounds into the trash bin and said, "Ah, memories."

# *Chapter 6*

Annoyed by Angelica's fond memories while she's releasing all contents of her stomach, she hurriedly attempts to clean herself up. She turns on the faucet and drinks straight from the tap, then pats her mouth dry. "I don't believe you!" Sofia says to Angelica while she puts the towel back on the counter. "I'm in agony expelling my guts and all you have to say is *Ah memories*," Sofia says quoting and mocking Angelica's previous remarks. "How's about here's a glass of water. Or let me hold your hair. Gah," Sofia rolls her eyes in annoyance and forgets all about where Angelica has brought her.

Angelica smiles at her and responds with, "Firstly, I do not sound like that. Secondly, maybe you should put all that focus into what lies before you."

With a quizzical stare, Sofia remembered that they had arrived at their first destination. The only problem was, she had no idea where she was. Angelica had taken them to a house that appeared to be old in age. The walls looked like they were made of wood, except you could tell it was fake. They had black stripes between each section of wood. The house smelled of smoke, as though someone smokes a pack a day and blows all the air directly into the ceiling which would explain the yellowish color. The furniture was dated, along with the cabinets. The home had an open floor plan to it, where the kitchen, dining room and living room shared the space.

"Where are we?" Sofia asked.

"We're exactly where we need to be," Angelica said in a mysterious tone.

Sofia questions the meaning of Angelica's statement, when in walks a woman from the hall. Her perfectly set brown curls laid across her shoulders but they did not hide what was written all over her face. She appears distraught, worrisome even. She has stress lines engraved between her furrowed brow, but not a single line to indicate that she smiles a lot. She begins making sure each item is in a precise location although there doesn't appear to be a mess of any kind. She is nervous, and it's making her stressed. She's pacing, checking her watch every few minutes. There's a ding and it's the timer for the oven. She sprints to it, taking out a hot casserole. She begins preparing the table for dinner, setting two places, and making sure everything is in perfect. Sofia stares at her watching every move she makes, but she cannot place her. She has never seen this woman before in her life.

"Who is she?" Sofia asks Angelica. "I've never met this woman in my life. What does she have to do with me?"

"Just watch and listen," Angelica tells her.

Sofia turns and watches her intently but all she does is nervously wait. Sofia looks around the room and there's not a single picture in the home. "Can she see us or hear us?" Sofia asks Angelica.

"No. No one will be able to, just as I told you before. We are part of a world that their minds keep them from seeing. They are broken and so is their ability to understand anything outside of themselves as most humans are suffocated by their own problems. Like a fish only being able to swim as far as the water will take him," Angelica replies.

Just then a car could be heard pulling into the driveway. The woman races to her feet and stands beside the table waiting to serve. As she gets into position, the doorknob turns, and a man walks in. Again, Sofia was left puzzled because she didn't know these people and the idea that her immortal soul was hanging in the balance because of these strangers, was ridiculous.

"Exactly how could I possibly be able to punish strangers?" Sofia asked furiously.

"Sometimes our punishments occur unknowingly. Not everything is blatant unlike that horrendous shirt you wear, that is obviously a cry for help. Or maybe you just like the attention. Either way, we get it. Now, pay attention," Angelica responded.

Sofia pulled at the corners of her red and black oversized shirt, when her thoughts of Angelica's insult was interrupted. A man soon entered the home, and he was dressed as if he had come home from a long day of work in what seemed to be construction. His white hard hat held underneath his arm, metal lunch box in hand, and steel toe boots with dried concrete on the tips. He had a look of disdain imprinted on his face, as if the years have permanently scared him physically marking several wrinkle lines. He held no kindness in his appearance and lacked any remanence of good looks. His scruffy jaw proved he did not care about proper grooming, which only accented his sour expression. One would think that a husband's return home would bring ease to his wife, but it clearly did not.

The woman stood at the table with a bright smile on her face, completely shedding any look of worry. She eagerly asked him questions such as, "How was your day, dear?", and "Can I get you anything?" While she looked like a happy homemaker, Sofia could see in her eyes that she was frightened, but of what or even worse…. who?

The man places his things down and finds his seat at the table. He says no words until his wife places his food in front of him. She pours him something to drink, helps with his napkin, and says, "Is there anything else I can get you?"

"No, dear. Why don't you have a seat, and we can enjoy our meal," the man replies.

Surprisingly happy, she takes her seat and begins to fix her own plate. Then her husband finally answers her question. "So, you wanted to know what I did today?" he asks. She nods in a cheerful manner, eager to hear his response.

"It was wonderful, Jo came to work today, because he's been gone since he broke his foot. He says he's finally on the mend, and said it was all because of you," he said with a sarcastic grin. "He told me you have been bringing him nice meals every day. That was sure nice of you," the man recalls to his wife as he eats. She notices a change in his voice, and Sofia and Angelica can sense something from her, it's not worry, it is terror, and her happy grin disappears.

Sofia clutches her chest and feels a sensation of panic, "Why is my chest beating so hard?" Sofia asks. "I feel so scared."

"It's wonderful isn't it. You are experiencing every emotion that she is feeling. Every. Single. Hint. I mean, haven't you always wanted others to understand how you feel? Now here's your moment to feel someone else's emotions," Angelica tells her cheerily as if she's just done a magic trick.

"So, this is how she's feeling?" Sofia questions. "Why is she so scared?"

"SHH! You really must listen, or you will never learn your lesson," Angelica reminded.

The man continued with his story saying, "You know, he said he came over the other day, to thank you for all your trouble. It's funny because you never mentioned it," he appeared to be upset, but his face was calm, and he never lost his grin.

Immediately the woman felt the need to explain, "He did, but he didn't stay for long. You were on your way home from work, and I-I was making you dinner. You work so hard and deserve to have nice meals. He came in for maybe a second or two, and he left. I didn't think that was big news or anything," she was so nervous. She swallowed hard in between sentences and stammered over her words.

"That is so nice of you Sarah," the man stated. "I do work hard, and I do deserve to have nice meals. But I'm surprised to find that you think that also?" he sat staring at her as he continued to eat. Feeling confused by his statement, Sarah tried to think about what she could have possibly done to upset him.

"I do think you deserve nice meals Sam. I do," she said quickly.

"Really, cause in that two second window that Jo was here, he said, you had an accident with my food. Do you happen to remember that?" Sam replied.

Sarah finally remembered what she had done. For a second her heart stopped, and she knew there was nothing that she could do or say to help herself. In a panic she spoke, "I dropped your chicken on the floor by accident, but it was raw, and I cleaned it up. I made sure it was completely good as new before I seasoned it the way you like it, a-and I made sure there was not a mess. Honest."

"That's not what he said. He said, you picked that cooked chicken up off the floor and placed it on my plate. Now, how come, Jo gets nice meals, but I must eat like a dog. DOGS EAT OFF THE FLOOR!" Sam said raising his voice and slamming his fists on the table.

"I'm sorry, Sam. I shouldn't have done that!" Sarah apologizes.

"SHOULDN'T HAVE DONE THAT?" Sam yells as he stands up firmly and flees toward Sarah with his chair flinging out from behind him.

He grabs her by the hair and asks, "What makes Jo better than me? Do you like him or something?"

The hate in his tone was gut wrenching. "No Sam. I only wanted to help him," she said crying.

"So, it's because you care more about him than me. You stupid...," Sam said in a tone of realization.

Standing back up and releasing her hair, he lifts his arm across his chest and hits her with the back of his hand. She's hit so hard she flies backward falling to the floor in her chair. His attack interrupts his own speech. Sofia's face feels swelled as she too was thrown backward. Not only could she feel Sarah's emotions, but she could feel the pain she was in too.

Sam began screaming, cussing, his rage had no filter and there was nothing anyone could do to stop him. Crying on the floor Sarah just cried out to him repeatedly saying, "I'm sorry, Sam!" He couldn't hear her over his own hateful words overpowering her voice as his rage drowned out everything but him.

"Why is he doing this?" Sofia asked with tear filled eyes picking herself up.

"You must listen," Angelica replies.

Suddenly, everything went quiet. Sofia could still see what was happening, but she couldn't hear or feel anything, until an angry voice filled her head. She was immediately filled with rage, thinking that Sarah needed to understand his pain, and that this was the only way. It had to be done. It was Sam's thoughts she was hearing, and you could tell that he felt his actions were justified. He felt that there was absolutely no other way.

Then a blow to her gut sent her flying back onto the floor, only this time she wasn't thinking hateful thoughts. She wasn't watching from the sidelines. She wasn't just feeling what Sarah was feeling. No, this time, she was Sarah.

Sam screamed and shouted, his spit shooting out of his mouth, sometimes in huge drops that fell onto her face. He kicked her over and over with his steel toe boot, as she lies crying in agony. She can no longer take any more blows to the gut. She must find a way to make it stop so she turns over. He slings his leg back once more and straight into her upper arm he hits, again, and again, and again. You would think that it would have been broken by now.

Sofia is still in her body, but she feels that she cannot move. Apparently, Sam feels as though she has now learned her lesson and ceases with his beating. He grabs her plate off the table and smashes it on the floor in front of her face sending pieces straight into her eyes and mouth. He wipes his brow and says, "If you think eating off the floor is okay, then have at it," he waits a second, and she doesn't move. Grabbing a handful of casserole in his hand and her hair in the other he pulls her up. He shoves the food into her mouth and demands that she eat it. "EAT YOUR DIRT FOOD!" he yells, and she begins to chew. She's crying as pieces of the china are digging into her gums. He waits for her to swallow and tosses her head to the ground.

He stands back up and takes a step to leave but turns around and reminds her, "Oh yea, don't you ever lie to me again. Now get up and clean yourself up. You need to go to the store and pick up some more dishes since you made me break the set. OH, and don't you leave looking like trash you disgusting waste of space. I don't understand how people at work endure you," He gathers himself and leaves to the back bedroom.

Sofia returns to Angelica's side as she's no longer in Sarah's body. She no longer feels any pain, but she sees Sarah still lying on the floor. In a fright she races to her side to see if she's okay. Sarah slowly moves taking it inch by inch. She's holding back her tears with all she has. She picks herself up and she begins to clean up the mess.

Sofia watches her intently, her heart aching for this woman she had never met. She's cleaning up after a man who nearly beat her to death over something as simple as a piece of food. She cleans it all up and it looks as though nothing had ever happened. She walks to her room and he's asleep on the bed. She quietly grabs her things, heads to the bathroom, and cleans herself up. Sofia begins to listen, to what is going through her head, and her thoughts are heartbreaking. This woman looked herself in the mirror and thought about how worthless she was. How unimportant to the world she is. No one cared for her.

Sofia cried quietly wondering how someone could make another person feel so useless. How could someone be so heartless? What makes someone so mean? "Why does she stay, Angelica?" Sofia asked watching Sarah to mend her broken wounds in a surprisingly professional manner.

"Emotions are complicated my dear. You see, if you feel like something makes you happy, you typically do that particular thing more often so you can feel more joy. However, when you think something isn't worth the effort, then you probably find ways to avoid it. Therefore, when a person is made to feel worthless, they don't feel that they are worth saving," Angelica explained.

Angelica watched Sofia as she cried for Sarah, and she could tell that she cared for her. "I know seeing this hurts you, and you feel very concerned for her, but there's nothing we can do," Angelica said.

Sofia felt annoyed because there was no point is showing her this. This experience was what was pointless and a waste of her time. "I don't understand why you're wasting my time showing me something so horrible that's happening to someone when there's nothing anyone can do about it. Not even a guardian angel will save her," Sofia spoke out in defeat. "What does this have to do with me?"

"Child, this has more to do with you than you think. Just because we don't know people doesn't mean that we don't affect them in some small way. Now don't get me wrong, I'm not saying that you're to blame for everyone in the world. However, for people that have some sort of connection with you, then you do," Angelica said.

"What connection? Look, I do feel for the woman, she shouldn't have to live like this, but I DON'T KNOW HER," Sofia enunciated. "Exactly how does this affect my soul?"

Angelica's bright golden wings appeared again, and she held out her hand and said, "Just wait love, there's more to see."

Sofia who had been keeping to Sarah's side, as she stood and cleaned, stepped closer to be wrapped in Angelica's wings for the next destination. While she was heartbroken for Sarah, her mind adjusted to new thoughts, when she remembered what happened last time. "I'm not going to throw up again, am I?" She asked.

Shrugging, Angelica replied, "You get used to it."

# *Chapter 7*

Once they arrived at their new destination and Sofia was released from Angelica's safe embrace, she felt light-headed and dizzy as she stumbled over each step she took. Reaching for the nearest wall so she could regain her balance. After a few short breaths to settle her head, she asked, "Get used to it, huh?"

When a response was not given, she looked around and realized that Angelica was nowhere to be found. Her equilibrium was settled, and the dizziness left, but she didn't understand where Angelica went to. She looked around and noticed she was in a crowd of people, carrying shopping bags. Through the abundance of people Angelica was not spotted but there were stores everywhere. Then she saw her, only it was not Angelica.

Sofia had been taken to the mall, on the same day as her accident. She knew this because walking towards her was someone she knew very well. It was herself.

She had the same clothes on as she currently did. The only difference was she looked upset and angry, and there was no love in her eyes. Looking at herself caused her mind to be flooded like a tsunami engulfing an entire city. Sofia could remember that day like a movie playing in her mind. Everything that had taken place was as vivid as she was. She could feel every emotion, remember every single thought, recall each decision, and it felt like it was happening all over again. After remembering how everyone made her feel, she questioned once again why this was her fault at all. She watched herself in slow motion, reading every inch of body movements and facial expressions she made, when…

"I told you that shirt was dreadful on you," Angelica said standing beside her as though she had been there the whole time. "Wow, I mean it really doesn't suit you. You should wear green, it really brings out your eyes. I mean unless you like the color of death, then I guess black is just your color. Am I right?"

Sofia jumped because Angelica's sudden rant came out of nowhere and scared her out of her own thoughts. Annoyed at

Angelica and her inappropriate timing, she asked her, "What are we doing here? This is the day of the accident, what did I do wrong here?"

"I told you we would be focusing on the events leading up to your accident, don't get frustrated with me. It's not my fault you don't pay attention. Also, none of this is about what you did wrong, this about making corrections for you to understand better," Angelica stated.

"But what does any of this have to do with Sarah. You know, the woman we just saw get beat half to death by her husband?" Sofia asked quizzically trying desperately to connect the dots.

Then in the distance Sofia heard a faint tone. Sofia recalled a familiar voice, only it was like music to her ears. There was not a more precious sound. It distracted her from her conversation with Angelica. She had to know where it was coming from. She looked through the crowd yet again, and there off in the distance was her mother. She was calling her "Sofia! Sofia!"

Hearing her mother shout across the way made Sofia melt. Her sweet voice pulled at her heart.

Despite feeling quite happy overhearing the sound of her mother's voice, considering she had longed to be near her. Sofia could not help but stare at her because there was something different about her. Something that she had never noticed. Sadness. She looked heartbroken.

"I hadn't noticed that about her. Why is she sad?" Sofia asked out loud to herself. "How come I couldn't hear this in her tone before. She sounds worried for me. I thought she was just mad."

"You probably couldn't hear her tone because you were too caught up in your own self-pity that you were unable to notice anything except yourself. Not to mention your lack of ability to realize your attitude was hurting those around you," Angelica stated.

Sofia thought to herself and realized that she had heard her mother calling her through the crowd, but she chose to ignore her. Mostly because she really didn't want to hear her. As far as missing the sound of her voice, well… she knew the answer. Frankly she didn't notice that she was sad because she was sad too. She didn't even notice that she was beginning to cry. This realization made Sofia feel sorry for how her mother was feeling and wishing she could make it better. She knew that feeling and she had no idea how to make that feeling go away. As she thought, her mind flipped from one side to the other, from her mom's feelings to hers. In an abrupt physical shake, hoping to end her racing thoughts, she landed on her last one ultimately siding with herself. This situation still wasn't her fault, she thought. She was upset, she was hurting too, didn't anyone care about her? Immediately feeling as though her feelings are just as valid, she did what she felt was best for the situation. She had… an outburst.

"You know what, I am entitled to my own feelings. Why doesn't someone check on me?" Sofia said in a disgruntled manner letting her thoughts run wild verbally.

"Well, it appears your mother is trying to do just that, but you won't allow her to. Will you?" Angelica said raising her eyebrow and tapping her finger on her chin. "But you are right though. Everyone is entitled to their own feelings, for instance how do you think that woman feels?" Angelica says making a sarcastic point as she starts pointing to a strange woman in the crowd.

She had on a long white dress, with a long sleeve ankle length cardigan, black gloves, and sunglasses. Her hair looked as though it was just recently fixed, and she looked sophisticated. "What does this woman have to do with me?" Sofia questioned.

"Why don't you have a closer look?" Angelica said. Then Sofia was transported to the woman's side, and everything was in slow motion. Each person took a minute to take half a step, but Sofia was able to move freely. It gave her a chance to examine the woman closely, and it didn't take long at all for Sofia to realize who she was. It was Sarah, the woman from the house.

She didn't look as though she was a battered wife, as a matter of fact, she looked amazing. Through her glasses Sofia could tell they were red from crying, and the long cover was hiding a large bruise that covered her left arm. What was she doing here at the mall Sofia wondered. Then Sarah stopped at a store window looking at the china being displayed, and Sofia realized exactly why she was here. The fresh bruise. The search for new dishes. The unrelenting shed of tears. Sofia could tell instantly. Sarah's incident had only just happened. Most likely before she had come here just as her husband had instructed her.

As she watched her pretend that her life was fine while admiring the china, Sofia remembered how she knew this woman. Her standing there, gave Sofia a déjà vu moment, and she knew she was the woman that bumped into her. She was the reason her mother had yelled at her that day. Just like that the dots were connected. Sofia wanted to be upset with her for causing her problems, but she couldn't shake the images of Sarah on the floor. The blows she endured, and the hatred thrust upon her.

"I can't believe she's able to just go about her day, like nothing happened. You would never think she was suffering like she is.

Or what that man did to her," Sofia said thinking out loud. All the while her frustration towards Sarah began to fade away.

Angelica appeared by her side and whispered into her ear. "He isn't the only one who caused her suffering that day," Angelica nods into the direction of Sofia walking through the crowd again. Their eyes watching each step Sofia makes when Angelica says, "How about a better seat?"

Sofia is then cast back into Sarah's body, just before her past self, bumps into her. Then as time returns to normal, Sarah is standing still, when something is thrust into her arm nearly pushing her over, sending sharp pains throughout her body. After as many blows as she had endured earlier, it feels as though this one impact could have been the one to finish her arm off. She turned and looked to see what it was that caused such harm and it was a petite girl with the angriest look on her face. She had no empathy or sympathy for what she had done. She said nothing, just a huff, a roll of the eyes, and a look that said I hate you. Sarah looked around and there was no one else in her way, she was either not paying attention or… her husband was right. She was a waste of space.

Then a woman appeared reaching her arms out gently holding her elbows in her hands. It was Sofia's mother. "I am so sorry.

Please excuse my daughter. Are you okay?"
she said attempting to look into her eyes but
could not see through her sunglasses.

Sofia could feel that Sarah's emotions
changed slightly as she listened. "She's
normally a sweet girl, she's just having a rough
day, and she's upset. I know it's probably my
fault, but she should never treat anyone this
way," Sofia's mother explained not only taking
the blame for Sofia but also hoping that Sarah
could be understanding of her teenage
daughter.

"It's fine. I'm hard to spot in a crowd.
Not really significant, you know," Sarah said in
a morose tone.

Her mother stopped and looked her
straight in the eyes, and said, "We are all
important. You are very significant. I'm truly
sorry."

Sofia could feel that Sarah started to
feel loved. It was a beautiful feeling to
experience in someone who didn't know love.
It was as if those few short words mended a
small crack in her heart that had been shattered
for so long.

Her mother sensing the hurt from Sarah,
sprinted in that moment to Sofia, grabbed her
by her arm, turned her around, and brought her
back to Sarah. "Sofia, apologize to this nice
woman." Her mother requested.

"Why? I didn't do anything to her," Sofia snapped back.

"You bumped into her, and it was rude," her mother explained still waiting for an apology.

"No, she bumped into me," Sofia stated radiating with a hateful vibe.

Both Sarah, and Sofia's mother could tell that there would not be an apology from the child who clearly was angry at the world. Sarah had endured those hateful glares every day of her life, and she could bear it no longer. She felt hated enough at home, she didn't need to be hated by a stranger too. She excused herself from the conversation, but as she left you could sense a feeling of depression and a lingering thought entered her mind, *he was right.*

With her leave Sofia was cast out of Sarah's body and watched herself walk away and head straight through the doors, with her mother racing after her. Turning around she looked at Sarah and felt saddened.

"But I… I didn't think I bumped into her that hard. It was so painful," Sofia said feeling guilty for her actions. "She was so hurt by it, not just emotionally but physically. She actually felt like I was perpetuating what her husband has been telling her, but I didn't say anything to confirm his statement. I didn't."

Sofia was confused because she had never met her before that day, and she didn't say anything to her at all. How could that one single moment cause someone to feel like a waste of space. How could she single handedly and unknowingly, help her husband put her down? There was nothing left to view, and everything around them began to fade away. Was Angelica, right? Was she the punisher?

# *Chapter 8*

All at once they appeared in the white empty room. Sofia could feel feelings of depression, heartbreak, sadness, pain. What she didn't feel was any type of joy or love. She felt like she was alone and that no one cared for her. She felt as if she were floating along on a dark river, where no one looked for her. No one missed her. More importantly, she wondered if she should end it all. Was this what she was feeling or was she experiencing what someone else was feeling? The strong emotions suffocated her bringing her down to her knees.

"What's wrong with me? Why am I feeling like this? Why am I thinking this way?" Sofia asked holding herself in her arms. They were overpowering her, and every ounce of strength she had was gone.

In a gentle tone Angelica said, "This is how Sarah is feeling right now. This is how she is feeling, thinking, and even dreaming. She hurts every minute of every day. Her life is so broken, that her mind cannot find any words to help put her back together again. Her mind is filled with self-hatred, and since she hasn't known love, she doesn't know how to love herself. Therefore, because you do not feel as though she is important, you must feel her pain."

Sofia then gets flashed into Sarah's mind, but the only thing there is darkness. She's standing there with a coldness coming over her. Every breath exhaled can be seen in a foggy smoke. Shivering, and curious as to what type of place fills Sarah's subconscious, she finds a similarity. She feels as though she has been sucked back where she first began and looking around... there is no way out.

Frantic, she hears a noise, and she begins searching. Far off in the distance she sees something. It's Sarah, and she's curled up in the floor. Only darkness surrounds her, and the pain that was inflicted upon her kept her pinned to the ground. It was then that Sofia understood that her brokenness kept her so beat-down that even her mental self could not pick herself up off the floor.

Sarah can feel her own body being drained from all happiness, joy, and love. She was being brought down by the very hateful voices that filled Sarah's mind. Every ounce of positive emotion that was stolen from her broke her bit by bit. She was slowly losing all will to live. Sofia could feel her body being wrenched with torturous strains. She needed to get out of there, but she had no idea how. She called out to Angelica, "Please, get me out of here!"

Returning from Sarah's mind, Sofia was overwhelmed by how Sarah's suicidal emotions were harming her. With her pulse racing she could tell she wasn't getting better even being out of Sarah's mind. Searching the depths of her soul, she found the last bit of fight she had and decided to fight with Angelica. She felt sorry for Sarah, she really did. But why should she suffer for someone else?

"Are you kidding me?" Sofia said raising her voice. "I didn't break her. I didn't cause her pain. This is not my fault."

Angelica watched as Sofia felt every inch of pain that Sarah had endured, and asked her a simple question, "Do you regret it?"

"What?" Sofia asked not understanding the question because as far as she was concerned her brokenness didn't begin with her.

"Do you regret your decisions made towards Sarah?" Angelica asked again.

"What decisions? Regret what?" Sofia asked once more annoyed at the insinuation that she had ill intentions towards Sarah. It was obvious that everything bad in her life had to do with her husband.

"I didn't do a thing to this woman, except bump into her. I admit that. I did. I was in the wrong when it comes to that. But how can I regret doing something that I had no idea would hurt her the way it did. What happened to her is horrible, but it was not my fault."

Angelica waited patiently for Sofia to end with her own rant because clearly, she didn't quite understand the point to this event. She worried that she was not going to be able to grasp the concept of her actions, and the entire point of this destination. She needed to get her to release herself of her selfishness, for her to see. As she thought of a plan of action, her thoughts were interrupted by a voice, clearly muffled by pain.

"Her husband is the one who should have to feel her pain. He's the one who wronged her. He's the one who hurt her. I didn't do a thing. I had one moment with her that's it!" Sofia shouted

That is when it hit Angelica. She knew exactly what how she needed to reach her to release her of her obvious blindness.

"Exactly," Angelica said with a smirk. "You had a moment. An opportunity. A chance, and what did you do? Did you show her kindness? Compassion? NO! You robbed yourself and her of any kind of love. You took that moment, and made a choice, a conscious decision not to. Instead, you decided to harm her even more, and why? Because you were too selfish to think of anyone but yourself."

"I didn't choose anything!" said Sofia. "I was upset, I didn't think. Don't my feelings matter?" She shouted her voice growing louder.

"Of course, your feelings matter, but are your feelings more important than someone else's?" Angelica asked waiting for a response.

Sofia couldn't argue with her in this moment, she was feeling awful and the emotions she was experiencing was growing into one singular pain in her chest. She hadn't known what a heart attack felt like, but she could only assume that it felt similar. There was no getting through any of this, she was in physical pain now, and Angelica was not going to see her side of the situation. Stressed and worried that this pain may never be relieved she let it all out on Angelica.

"THIS IS RIDICULOUS!" Sofia Screams. "I don't want to do this anymore. Where's my mom? Take me home, NOW!"

Angelica looks into her eyes and asks her, "Why do you give up so easily? Is it because you know you're wrong, or because you can't handle the pain that comes with it?"

"I'm not giving up. I'm in a lot of pain. Please, I'm sorry." Sofia pleas.

"So, then you admit that you were the one in the wrong?" Angelica asks happily as though she has won a game.

"NO, I wasn't the one in the wrong, but I was wrong. Please, make it stop, I'm hurting," Sofia begs.

Beginning to get frustrated with Sofia's selfishness. Her insistent refusal to take accountability for her actions was infuriating. How could she help her if she was too stubborn to learn from her mistakes? She decides to try one more time, before she concludes that she has failed. As she thinks of another tactic, she watches Sofia in pain grabbing her chest. She could tell that it was becoming more intense with every second. She thought and thought, and Sofia began to cry. Then it hit her, the angle she had before was wrong, but this one, was going to be the one to save her.

She knelt beside Sofia and asked her one last question. "You say, you didn't choose. You say, you were in pain too. You say, you only had one moment," Angelica said watching Sofia's eyes glare up to her. "Your mother had one moment too. She was hurting too. I ask you; how did she handle the moment?"

With the thought of her mother, Sofia began to think about what her mother said to Sarah when she interacted with her. She was sad, and her heart was breaking but she never said a hurtful word to her. Her mother was heartbroken as well, but instead of focusing on her own problems, she stopped, and chose to show her love, in a moment where her mother needed love too. She even took the moment to remind her how important she is. She was helpful, thoughtful, encouraging, and kind. Sofia remembered how Sarah felt in their moment together, and she remembered how her mother made her feel loved. Sofia knew there was no arguing with Angelica any longer because she was right. She did have a choice. The same one her mom had, only she handled it differently. While her mother was focused on Sarah's pain, Sofia was focused solely on her own. There was no reason for it, and all she had to do was make one small apology. She began to feel guilty. Sad rather, because she knew she was the one in the wrong. Despite her views on the situation, and her stubborn reasons... she was completely wrong.

The guilt began to weigh on her, but oddly the pain in her chest began to lessen. She was beginning to feel better, even though she felt worse about her actions. Her alleviating pain was a beautiful sight to Angelica because she could tell that she was beginning to see the light.

"You're right. I could have been nicer to her," Sofia said quietly looking up at Angelica. "Or... I *should* have been." As she admitted her actions were not justified, she could feel the pain subside completely. With no pain in sight, her mind cleared, and she wondered about her mom.

"Does everyone who dies, or is dying have to go through this?" Sofia asked.

"No," Angelica replied. "This is only for special circumstances and your mother is not one of them."

"What do you mean?" Sofia asked wondering what would make her bring up her mom.

"I know you're wondering if she had to experience this too. Don't worry, your mother is fine where she is," Angelica said assuring. She has a heart filled with love; I mean just look how she treated Sarah.

Sofia felt exhausted by all the recent events but felt better knowing her mother didn't have to endure such pain. This destination caused her to feel as though she were dying physically, and it was not something she wanted to experience again. Angelica stood to the side of her as she was deep in thought, and reached out her hand again, signaling their time to leave. Reaching for her hand, Sofia quickly pulled back.

"Wait, did I learn my lesson?" Sofia asked hoping that it was all over.

"Well, what did you learn?" Angelica asked.

"Umm, to watch what you say to people because sometimes the things we say, or even don't say can cause harm," Sofia replied in a questionable tone.

"That sounds like a pretty good lesson, my dear," Angelica said smiling. "Maybe the next destination will help you understand better. So, you are not questioning if you've learned the right lesson, though," Angelica said motioning for her to take her hand yet again.

Sofia took her hand in hers and quietly hoped that the next lesson would be easier to watch or at the very least, wouldn't hurt near as much.

# *Chapter 9*

As they arrived, Sofia stood against Angelica with her wings wrapped around her in loving warmth and she couldn't kick the feeling that they were somewhere very familiar. After her last experience with Sarah, her mind raced with a lot of concerns. What would she feel? Who would it be? Would she be able to learn this lesson?

She opened her eyes and her heart filled with joy. She was home. The smell of mom's coffee filled the air. Her sewing kit was still left out by the couch because her shirt needed to be mended. The clothes were left out along the couch because she had spent all day yesterday doing laundry but ran out of time to put it all away. Her antiques set on the shelves and Sofia thought of the stories she shared of each of them. She even displayed the rocks her and her sister had brought her over the years because she said it was the greatest gift of love. There were remnants of her mother all throughout their house, and she wondered what it was going to be like to never see that again.

Admiring the home her mother made for them, her thoughts had been interrupted. Behind her was the sound of a glass shattering against their concrete floor. Only a few seconds past before you could hear a voice shout, "What happened?" It was the voice of her mother.

Sofia ran into the kitchen where the sound had echoed from, and she saw herself standing there in front of her mother. Sofia remembered what event was taking place. It was the morning of their accident.

Her mother's question annoyed her, obviously because Sofia did not answer except in sighs and grunts.

"Excuse me, I asked you a question," her mother stated. Still, no verbal response was given.

"Step to the side and watch your step. You don't want to get glass in your feet." Her mother's voice never raised, but Sofia could feel herself being angered.

"Looks like you broke your voice along with the glass huh," Angelica said trying to make a joke as she appeared by Sofia's side.

"My voice is fine," Sofia said. "I was just annoyed, because I knew she would over-react, like she always does. It's just a stupid glass."

"Right, so rolling your eyes, and huffing and puffing is how you get her to understand how this accident happened? Wow, you are not the brightest crayon in the box now, are you?" Angelica said sarcastically.

With Angelica trying to alleviate some of the tenseness in the room, they continued to listen to the conversation between mother and daughter. "It's not that big of a deal. I didn't know someone put that glass there. I put this box on the counter and it fell off," Sofia told her mother.

"So, you weren't paying attention," Her mother said.

"Ugh. No, I was. I just didn't see it," Sofia said back.

"We have an entire kitchen of counter space, and you manage to knock over the one glass, or item for that matter, left out on the counter?" Her mother argued.

"I didn't mean to!" Sofia said in a snarky tone.

"How about, I'm sorry mom. I should've paid more attention mom. Let me help you mom. Anything other than those grunts you claim to be words," her mother requested.

"Whatever, do you want help?" Sofia said in an irritable tone with her body language suggesting that she didn't want anything to do with her mother.

Feeling the irritable vibes cascading off her daughter, Sofia's mother realized that forcing her to help would probably end in her sweeping angrily and spreading the broken glass. Even worse she'd be too angry to be careful and cut herself. No. It would be safer to refuse her ingenuine offer.

"No. Just please be more careful next time. Glass ware costs money and there's going to be a time when even one dollar is too much to spare," her mother told her.

With that Sofia took the offer to leave the room. As she left, Sofia watched herself leave to her bedroom and felt how frustrated she was getting. She could feel the annoyance she held toward her mother, and remembered it being justified. Unfortunately, she remembered their argument to be much worse in her mind than it was. She remembered there being a lot of yelling from her mother, but she never raised her voice. She remembered her mother jumping down her throat the moment she heard the glass breaking. Hmm… maybe it wasn't justified like she thought. Maybe her mother wasn't the one in the wrong. Maybe the one in the wrong… was her.

Pondering her memories and the accuracy of them she followed herself to the room, where she sat alone and irritated. Sofia sat beside herself on her floor by her bed, taking in the emotions she was experiencing. She felt alone, uncared for, and hated. She couldn't believe her mother would be so upset over something so small, that she sat and wished she wouldn't have to deal with her short temper again.

Absorbing all these emotions, Sofia couldn't help but think that her emotions were invalid. Her mother didn't make her feel this way, these feelings came out of her own interpretation. Why would she take something so small and turn it into something big. They sat there together. Alive Sofia with her mother's lack of care for her, and dead Sofia's frustration for herself. Both of their emotions rising in confusion. When in walks a child, with curly brown pig tails, and a box full of crayons in one hand and a coloring book in the other. It was her younger sister, Isabella.

"Sofia, can you color with me?" she asked.

"No. I don't want to," Sofia replied.

"Please, I really like to color with you," her sister said.

"No! Leave me alone," Sofia said sternly.

"Just one picture?" her sister asked again.

"I said NO," Sofia shouted.

"But I promise it will be really quick. I just want to spend time with you. Please, Sofia?" her sister begged.

In that moment Sofia felt an intensity of rage burning in the pit of her stomach. She had no control over what was about to come out of her mouth like a fire gone out of control. Everything she was feeling came out in a ball of hateful words fueled by fire. The wrath was unleashed, and her sister was the one who would take the hit.

"WILL YOU LEAVE ME ALONE! I DON'T WANT TO SPEND TIME WITH YOU! YOU'RE ANNOYING! GO AWAY! I DON'T WANT TO COLOR WITH YOU BECAUSE I DON'T LIKE YOU! NO ONE LIKES YOU! YOU'RE SUCH A BRAT SOMETIMES! NOW LEAVE!" Sofia screamed at Isabella.

With tears in her eyes, she walked away slowly and left her room. Sofia could sense feelings of being a burden from her sister and couldn't believe that a five-year-old could have emotions like that. Or, that she would be the cause of it.

"And the sister of the year award goes to…. SOFIA!" Angelica said like she was announcing the winner at the tony awards. She began making cheering sounds for background effect as Sofia sat feeling guilty for making her sister feel so badly.

"You really put that five-year-old in her place," Angelica said.

"I didn't know I hurt her feelings like that," Sofia said worriedly.

Angelica stood with a puzzling look on her face, tapping her chin and said, "hmm, you didn't know that saying *'no one likes you'* would hurt her feelings? Hmm, you're right. I don't think anyone saw that coming."

Sofia rolled her eyes at Angelica as she pointed out the obvious, but she truly felt that she had no idea. While thinking about the events that took place she wondered if she was in the wrong this time too. She over-reacted about her mom, and she hurt her sister more than she thought she did. Although, until now, she couldn't remember half of what she had said to her sister either. Her thoughts entranced her, as she forgot where she was, and then suddenly heard her mother call her to leave.

Following herself out the door, to leave with her mom, Sofia walked outside, and everything disappeared. There was nothing but a white room. She turned around and the door to their home was still there. Concerned, she walked back in, and she was back in her home with Angelica waiting on her.

"Where did they go?" Sofia asked Angelica.

"You are not meant to follow them. The place meant for you is here. This is where you must learn your lesson," Angelica explained. "I mean, I guess you could learn something from following them, but what all can you learn from a solid white room?"

"But what's here for me to learn? I left with mom," said Sofia.

Then a voice traveled throughout the house. It was her dad calling to her sister reminding her he was just outside if she needed him or wanted to come and play. That's when Sofia remembered, and relief set in.

"That's right we left her at the house with dad," Sofia said happily remembering that both Angelica and her mom insisted that she had hurt Isabella's feelings. "If she has him to play with, there's no way she's still upset over something I said, that doesn't matter."

"What makes you think what you say doesn't matter to her?" Angelica asks.

"Because she's five. She'll get to playing and forget all about what I said," Sofia insisted.

"Well, why don't we check in on her and find out," Angelica stated.

Into her room they went, to find Isabella coloring in the floor of her room.

"See, she's fine. Already forgot all about..." Sofia started to say until she heard a quiet noise.

It sounded small but came in waves. It resembled laughing but in a painful kind of way. The closer she walked towards Isabella, the louder the sound became. Kneeling beside her sister, she realized what she was hearing. Her sister was crying. Isabella had taken refuge in her room, coloring a picture of a girl with blue scribbled lines coming from her eyes. She couldn't be consoled because she wouldn't stop repeating the words that were spoken to her.

"Go away. No one likes you. You're a brat," she said her tears dropping onto her picture.

The longer she said it, the more she cried. The more she cried the more Sofia could feel that she believed it. She could feel her little sister's heart beating rapidly. Her thoughts racing with pictures of people hating her. She felt like she wasn't worth anyone's time. Sofia felt so awful for how her sister felt and reached to give her a hug to make her feel better, but she couldn't. She knew what she was repeating was what she had said to her, and nothing she did would take them back now. She had no idea that one outburst could harm her emotionally the way that it did.

Angelica walked up beside her and took her hands. She helped Sofia up to her feet and asked, "Does it make you regret what you said?"

"I mean, I guess I shouldn't have said it, but it's not like I did it knowing that this would happen," Sofia answered.

"So, you regret it, but you don't think it was entirely your fault?" Angelica said exhausted.

"It was my fault because I said it. But I still think she will get over it soon enough, I mean, how long can a five-year-old remember something like this? It's not like it will scar her for life or anything," Sofia expressed.

"So, five more minutes and she'll be done," Angelica asked.

"Yes," Sofia said confidently.

Angelica then locked eyes with Sofia while they were hand in hand and waited five minutes. They looked over at Isabella still on the floor but now she was asleep with tear-stained cheeks.

"Okay, so maybe a little longer than five minutes, but you see she's already put herself to sleep," Sofia said as though she had made her point.

Angelica looked at her with a smile growing twice as big, and says, "Sometimes time passes too quickly for anyone to notice and before they know it, time has flown." With that statement she turns and looks back at

Isabella. Sofia follows her lead and looks too, but Isabella is gone.

"Where did she go?" Sofia asked confused. "And who is this?"

Angelica simply backs away from her to allow Sofia to investigate. There's another kid in her room, sitting where Isabella once sat. The room looked almost the same but different pictures on the wall and a butterfly comforter on the bed. It wasn't as cheery as it once was. There was now a sadness in the room. There was a machine next to be bed, and furniture was minimal. Sofia had no clue who this girl was, but she was older, and skinnier. She sat on the floor coloring pictures and being perfectly quiet. Sofia looked around moving towards the side of her to get a look at her face when the little girl reached her hand to her head. She had an itch which apparently was severe because she scratched so hard that she knocked off her wig. The child was bald.

Sofia's heart began to sink because she knew exactly what this meant for the little girl. Her skin was pale all over, as if she had been sick for a while unable to go outside. Feeling sorry for her, she went and took a seat in front of her. Sofia closed her eyes and began to feel what she was enduring. She was tired, sick. She ached all over and prayed for her life to end. She was depressed, lonely, and felt like a burden.

"Who is this kid?" Sofia asked opening her eyes.

"Look into her eyes," Angelica suggested.

Sofia sat waiting for the girl to look up from her drawings, and when she did, it didn't take long for Sofia to realize that this child.... Was her sister.

# *Chapter 10*

Her eyes had dark circles around them, and they glared with pain. For a child who once held a lot of light in her eyes, there was none there today. Sickness could be read all over her face, from the pale skin, and the weak movements. No matter what she did, there was nothing to mask it. Not even her wig remained on her head to hide the truth. Sofia had never seen or met someone who suffered from cancer, but she knew without a doubt, that this had to be the reason why her sister was sick. Her eyes began to well with tears, as she realized that there was a chance that her sister may not survive her illness, and she needed to know the exact name of her executioner.

"What kind of cancer does she have?" Sofia asked Angelica.

"Renal cell carcinoma. A year ago, she was diagnosed, and the cells had spread to her other organs. They said if they had known years ago, a simple transplant would've saved her from this," Angelica gently replied. "In case you are wondering, your mother was not a match. While your father was, he unfortunately was turned away due to his diabetes."

Sofia hearing this news burst into tears hanging her head down low into her knees. She couldn't imagine life without her little sister, there was no way possible that something like this would happen to her. She was always so sweet, and innocent. She was overwhelmed with heartache, and she felt she needed answers.

"Why is she sick? How could this happen to her? She's never done a thing wrong," Sofia asked urgently.

"This world is filled with sickness, my dear, and sometimes it's hard for us all to understand," Angelica attempted to explain with a heavy heart. "There's no specific reason as to *why* these things happen, they just do because the world is a broken place."

Sofia's heart didn't feel any better with the answers she received. She only felt worse. Like there was nothing that anyone could do to help her. She hung her head down in despair and could think nothing more than the beauty that was her little sister. She didn't deserve this, and deep-down Sofia wished it had been her instead. The frustration of feeling insufficient was beginning to feel like rage. She was mad, defeated, and helpless. Her crying interrupted by the thought that there *was* someone who could help. There was someone who could save her; and she was standing right beside her.

Her crying ceased for a second as her eyes drew upward to make eye contact and she began to plead with Angelica, "Can't you do something? Can't you heal her? Why is God not healing her?" Sofia started to scream in a shaky voice. Her crying was making it difficult for her to speak in an enunciated manner.

"That is not a question for me to answer. It's also not a question you need to ask," Angelica responded.

Sofia wanted desperately to help her sister, to hug her, hold her, tell her it would all be okay. But when she reached for her, her arms faded through her, and all she could feel was air. She only wanted to assure her she was there for her. Since she could not hold her, she was only left staring at her with only her memories of their time together. With her last memory Sofia remembered her hateful words spoken to Isabella on the day of her accident. The dread in her heart to know that it would not matter if she made a mend with her sister now or not was building. She needed to ask the only question important to her in this moment.

"Does she know I didn't mean it?" Sofia asked with tears streaming down her face.

"You didn't mean what?" Angelica questioned.

"Does she know that I don't think she's a brat. That she's not annoying. That I want her with me always," Sofia cried out. With her deepest sob she said, "Does she still know that I love her?"

Angelica gave her a moment to quiet her tears, as she answered her questions, "No, I'm afraid, in this scenario you died on the day of the car crash and were unable to speak to her before. The last words she ever heard you say, left her crying in her room alone."

To hear that your last words to someone broke their heart was one of the most difficult things to ever hear possibly. Sofia couldn't express the amount of hurt she felt. She realized that those last words weren't washed away. It didn't matter that Isabella was only five. Those words were what she was going to remember forever, because they hurt her, and because they were the last memory, she had of her big sister.

As Sofia cried, Isabella began to look weak. Something was wrong. Her eyes rolled back, and her body collapsed to the floor. "Bella!" Sofia called. "Isabella!"

The machine began to chime loudly echoing throughout the house. Her mother, father, and a nurse rushed into the room quickly checking her vitals, and sticking needles into her IV. Sofia was in terror to watch her little sister helpless. Slowly she backed away to make room for them all as they rushed to tend to her needs. She found herself in the corner of the room watching the nightmare escalate. What if her sister didn't make it, she thought. Their father grabbed their mother, pulling her to his side as they stood crying. Isabella was unresponsive and the nurse had begun CPR hoping to bring her back. Her worry rose when all of a sudden, a breath was taken by Isabella and the glorious chime from the monitor began to beat again signaling a strong heartbeat. She was back, and ready to be placed back in her bed.

Relieved Sofia let out tears of praise, she was in a joyous mood. Her sister was still alive, and there was not a better feeling.

"She's okay! She's Okay!" Sofia shouted in excitement to Angelica. "Did you see her? She's so strong."

"Yes, I saw her, and she is. But did you notice them?" Angelica turned her eyes toward the adults in the room.

They appeared concerned, as though this was not a time for excitement as Sofia thought. Why weren't they as excited as she was, Sofia thought to herself.

"Angelica, why are they worried? Is Isabella getting better or worse?" Sofia asked.

"Unfortunately, your sister hasn't ever had much of a positive outlook towards herself since you died and going through Chemo hasn't helped." Angelica explained.

"What do you mean?" Sofia asked confused.

"Well, in this scenario it's important to be encouraged, and positivity helps motivate the body and soul to want to heal and want to fight. In Isabella's case, she has neither. You see, you left her with an emptiness that cannot be filled. She hears her mother and father fight about money, about how they already lost a daughter. In her loneliness she remembers the words you spoke to her. Unfortunately, for her, she agrees with you. Not only does she not want to be a burden, she also doesn't want your parents to go in debt taking care of someone who no one cares for anyway," Angelica told her.

Waiting for Sofia to catch on, Angelica realizes she has to explain further. "She feels like a burden on those around her, and those thoughts have led her to believe that they would be better without her. So hey, I guess your words that just *needed to be said,* gave her an outlook to focus on for the rest of her days. Not that she has many left to live."

Listening to Angelica, Sofia walks slowly to her sister's bedside, and with that last statement of Angelicas her spirit feels crushed. She never intended for this to happen. She was upset, and she let it take control of her instead of her controlling it. Now her sister was sick and had no fight left in her. Sofia breathed deeply and felt everything inside of her build. She could feel strength inside her, and she reached for her sister's hand and for some reason she was able to hold her hand in hers.

Astounded that she was able to hold her hand when she couldn't even hug her before, Sofia fell to her knees at Isabella's bedside. Grasping tightly to her hand she knelt and took a second to pray. She hoped she could hear what she had to say, or at least feel her next to her

Sofia began to speak but a pain in her chest began to build. She ached, and the pain grew to such intensities that the tears flowing down her cheeks were both from the pain she felt from her sick sister, and from the agony of her internal pain. Sofia knew she needed to speak to her sister, despite the pain she was feeling, her sister needed to know. She built up what power she had in herself and began to let it all out.

"Isabella, I love you. I love you more than I love myself. You're not a brat. I want you around me all the time because the best

times I've had were spent with you. The day
God made you my sister, was the best day of
my life, and I remember it clear as day," Sofia
said crying softly. She placed her sister's hand
against her cheek and said to her, "Please don't
die. Live. You're a gift, and this world would
be robbed without the light you bring to it."

As Sofia spoke to her sister, the pain in
her chest continued to grow. She could feel her
heart tearing apart.

Angelica could feel a tug at her own
heart strings, but she had a job to do, and the
lessons must be learned. As Sofia poured her
heart out to her sister, Angelica interrupted the
heartfelt moment to bring clarity to the
situation and let the lesson be revealed.

"For someone who thinks that *she'll
just get over it*, it sure doesn't seem like you
feel that way now?" Angelica stated hoping it
would spark a fire of epiphany.

Sofia turned in frustration at Angelica
while sitting beside her sister. With everything
going on, and her having to watch her sister
die, how could she bring up such things.

"I love my sister. I may get mad, but I
love her no matter what," Sofia said attempting
to shout clenching her chest with her other
hand.

She turned back and sat in silence as
she looked into her sisters' painful eyes.
Understanding that there was nothing she could

do, except one thing. She leaned in and whispered, "I take it back."

With a smile on her face, Angelica said calmly, "Sounds like someone might be learning these lessons after all."

With those words, Sofia could no longer feel any pain in her chest, but the heartbreak was still there.

Angelica slowly walked to Sofia, her wings opening. She knelt beside her with her wings ready to wrap around Sofia once more, when Sofia said, "Don't make me leave her."

"You're always with her," Angelica replied taking Sofia into her embrace.

The warm feeling comforted her, and the bright light surrounded her. They were on their way to the next place, but how could Sofia focus on anything after everything she just witnessed. Her sister was dying, and she had no desire to fight at all because what she had said. Sofia felt so guilty the thought of not continuing with her own lessons seemed like a good idea. Afterall, with what happened with her sister, she felt she deserved an eternity in hell.

Through the few seconds she was wrapped in Angelica's wings, she remembered that the only way to be with her again would be to continue.

Fear set in, when she realized she would have one last lesson to learn, which meant another place to explore. She wondered if their next destination would be easier or worse to endure. Looking up to Angelica she prayed for easier.

# *Chapter 11*

The light began to fade, and her tear-filled eyes struggled to make out the images appearing before her. There was nothing around familiar, and Sofia knew that they were somewhere new yet again. Knowing she had never been here before; she searched her mind for a reason why they would be here. What stranger did she affect this time?

Looking around the room there were instruments, metronomes, music stands, and she realized where she was. It was a band hall, one that you would find in a high school, although she could not recall this particular one. Scanning the room for something familiar, a light had suddenly turned on in the corner of the room. Beneath the light, was emptiness. There was only the shimmer of the dust particles settling. Intrigued, Sofia looked around to see what caused the light to turn on. After searching, she returned her glance back to the light, but this time, there was someone there. It was a boy, he had red hair, and he was sitting on a stool playing the guitar. As he sat playing, he looked up and Sofia knew who he was instantly.

"Dad? That's my dad!" Sofia said proudly. "Hey, Angelica, that's my dad. He's so young. I don't ever remember him being so young."

Sofia stared at him letting the joy of seeing her dad wash away the painful memories of her sister.

"Maybe, that's because this was before you were born," Angelica said appearing beside her.

No wonder he looked so young, she thought. Sofia was overtaken by the sight of her father, and she was entranced by his youth, as well as his playing.

"He's not playing as well as he does now, but I know that's him," Sofia said proudly.

However, her proud moment was stolen when suddenly she started thinking about every place, they had gone prior, was due to some kind of wrongful act perpetuated by her. But she couldn't remember having any type of argument, let alone small discussion with her father on the day of her accident.

"Wait, what lesson do I have to learn from my dad?" Sofia asked.

"Maybe the lesson has little to do with your father, and a lot to do with someone else," Angelica said vaguely.

Just as Angelica finished her sentence, Sofia noticed her dad looking up again. Only this time he had a twinkle in his green eyes that he was giving to the girl in front of him, only it was not Sofia. Standing beside Sofia was a girl with long black hair who was listening intently. Sofia knew without hesitation that she had been standing beside… her mom.

"Mom," Sofia said in a hushed tone. "That's my mom." Her eyes were widened because she couldn't believe what she was seeing. Her mother was so young. She seemed innocent and kind. Just seeing her mother made her so happy, but it also rose questions. Sofia asked herself why she would need to be here when this was before her time? What relevance does this have regarding her?

Unable to answer these confusing thoughts, she decided to ask Angelica again. "So, if it's not my dad, then it's my mom… right?"

Without a word, Angelica looked at her with a smile. Sofia could tell that it was her mother who she needed to learn this last lesson from.

Sofia took a moment and asked, "If I'm supposed to learn the lesson from my mother, then why am I here before I was born? What does that have to do with me?"

Angelica decided to explain things without giving the lesson away. "Things that don't involve us, have a way of affecting us. Isn't it interesting how things can affect us without us knowing?" Angelica responded.

"I don't follow," Sofia responded quizzically.

"Now it's time to watch," Angelica suggested as she exasperatingly turned back towards the couple.

Sofia turned her gaze back toward her mother and father, as she watched them take each other into a warm embrace. As the seconds passed, she could see a love between the two that grew. Soon the remix of their relationship and their life together began to play out. The video montage of their greatest hits flashed before them, as if they were standing in a dark room in front of a movie theater screen. All remnants of the band hall where they once stood, had disappeared. Only the screen could be seen.

Sofia watched their very first date. She saw them dance. She watched them sitting around a fire on a cold night. Their love was growing, and she found herself staring solely at her mother. There was something different about her, something she had never seen. Her mother was excited, and not an excited like she was when she changed her first tire or fixed the plumbing in the house without any help. No, this was a different excitement. As she searched her mind for what it could be that made her mother glow, she unintentionally found herself speaking aloud, "Why is she so excited?"

"There's something about your mother that you may not know," Angelica stated in a mysterious manner.

"What?" Sofia asked, "What don't I know?"

"Your mother had an excitement for life," Angelica said, smiling at her mother. Standing before her, her father slowly faded out of the picture.

Moments of her mother's life began to play, and she found something she never knew. Her mother had goals that surpassed the goals of her family. She prayed to go further than her parents before her and give them what they always desired. Her dreams were so intricate that she gathered information about the military, applied to colleges, created a five-year plan, but… she was young, and she wanted to enjoy her youth while she still had it.

Sofia watched her mother ask her own father if she could take a year off work to take time for herself. She was worried that this would be the last chance she would have before life would whisk her away.

Sofia began to look puzzled. "I don't understand?" she took a silent pause. "Mom wasn't in the military, nor did she go to college. If she was excited for life, and this was what she was excited for... why didn't she do them?"

Angelica reached her hand out to her, and explained as best she could, "Sometimes, our plans do not align with our actions. People can be excited about future events but create obstacles for themselves along the way."

"Obstacles?" Sofia said thinking out loud.

The picture they had been viewing began to play again. Only this time, the excitement they had once seen on her mother's face had vanished. The look on her face couldn't be described to any expression. She simply appeared lost.

"What's wrong?" Sofia asked staring deeply at her mother trying to solve the puzzle. "Her excitement is gone."

Angelica could only stand in the back and wait for her to watch further. Her father entered the room, and he appeared just as lost as she was. The words spoken between them after minutes of pure uninterrupted silence was more confusing to Sofia than their lack of excitement. Her father spoke first, "What now?"

"I don't know," her mother said quietly.

"Angelica, what's going on?" Sofia asked worriedly. "Why do they seem lost, disappointed, as if their whole life has changed somehow? Did someone die?"

"No," Angelica reassured her. "No one has died. Someone lives."

"Lives?" Sofia asked. "What does that mean?"

Angelica gave her a moment, and then said, "You're a very smart girl. Why don't you rack that beautiful brain in that marvelous red head of yours and think what would make two young teenagers who were once excited about their future, completely worried about what the future holds? All because of the life of another."

Sofia thought and thought, until she knew exactly what would cause them to question everything, and suddenly be worried about their future.

She was watching the very moment her mother found out that she was pregnant... with her.

"They're disappointed because of me," Sofia said in a whispering tone. "I stole their excitement."

"No, my dear," Angelica interjected. "It's not that they were disappointed, it's that they had no idea how to handle it. For example, if you're driving to a place and you know the road to take to get there, but there's a traffic jam, you must take an alternative road. This can cause you to be worried if it will get you where you're supposed to be, because nothing looks the same. Does that make sense?"

"You're saying that they want me, they just worry that the path they wanted to take is going to change a little. They're worried about the road ahead," Sofia calmly explained Angelica's analogy.

"Exactly. I knew you were a smart one," Angelica replied happily.

"So, do they ever get excited about me, or at the very least…Does my mom?" Sofia asked staring in the face of her mother, desperately hoping the answer is yes.

"Why don't you take a closer look," Angelica said in a mystifying tone.

Suddenly the picture of her mother turned into grains of sand that were carried away by a gust of wind. They circled around her as though she were in the eye of a tornado, and she could hear nothing, but the roaring of the wind. In an instant the sand tornado tightened to her body, and Sofia was losing breath. Her chest began to ache, and her heartbeat lowered. Then as the roar grew and the howling screeched, Sofia fell to her knees and there was an explosion. The sand fell to the ground, and there was silence. Nothing could be heard or seen, and in the remnants of the pile of sand, Sofia's body could not be found.

Waking from the explosion she opened her eyes. She could see she wasn't in the same place, there was no dark room, but there were lights all around. The sand that had once surrounded her, was replaced with people. She had no idea where she had appeared, only that she was scared, and desperately longed for some kind of comfort.

Sofia could feel herself being cradled but couldn't control what was happening. She felt as if she had lost her ability to speak. It was as if she had no control over her own body let alone her vocal response. The light shining into her eyes made it difficult to open, her eyes pained as though they were sensitive to light.

As the moments passed, she could feel her body being shifted. She had no idea what was happening, and the terror was beginning to build. She didn't know where she was, she was unable to speak, and she couldn't see anything. All she could do was cry.

As Sofia cried, hoping someone would rescue her. She felt an immediate feeling of comfort. The feeling of security was evident, and through each inhale of oxygen she could smell something familiar. It was intoxicating, it filled her lungs and radiated into her body. The warmth was incredible, and she felt the desire to see what was responsible for this wondrous feeling.

Slowly she opened her eyes and there before her was a face she could never mistake. Sofia looked into the eyes of her mother. This was the day Sofia had been born. Their connection was so powerful, nothing could have broken it. Her mother's voice was soft but passionate. As Sofia rested in the arms of her mother, she saw it. The excitement that was once gone, was visible again. Her mother was excited for life, and she was going to get to be a part of it.

Sofia felt so thankful, knowing that her mother had excitement about her, that she released a smile. That smiled made her mother smile, and then she heard the first words to her from her mother.

"You're mine, and I am yours. There's nothing I wouldn't give for you. Until my last days, until my last breath, I will sacrifice my life for you," Her mother spoke to her, as though she were speaking into Sofia's soul.

Their connection was solidified, and Sofia felt closer to her mother more than ever.

As quickly as she entered her newborn body, she was brought back before Angelica. Sofia fell into her arms sobbing.

"Why are you sad?" Angelica asked.

"I'm not sad, I am happy," Sofia replied. "She loves me."

"Of course, she loves you," Angelica stated patting Sofia on the back. "She wouldn't put up with all your crap if she didn't."

Immediately Sofia stopped crying, as Angelica's harsh words of reality set in.

In an attempt to take Angelica's crude words out of her mind, Sofia thought for a moment. Then realized that if her mother, loved her and was excited for her, why didn't she continue with her plans? Why did her future change?

"Angelica," Sofia asked. "Why didn't mom, go through with her plans?"

Angelica raised her head and looked to the sky to find the right words and then said, "Sometimes, the future we want, isn't the future we get. In your mother's case, you were worth the trade."

# *Chapter 12*

Sofia didn't know how to interpret that comment. What did Angelica mean that *she was worth the trade*? Standing there pondering her guardian Angel's peculiar reflection of her mother's decisions in her life, Angelica took her moment of silence to wrap her in her beautiful wings yet again.

When her wings opened, Sofia's curiosity dwindled as new curiosities took residence in her mind. The room was dark, and there was nothing around except a simple light shining down on her mother. She was alone in her room, crying begging God to make him love her. The sight was despairing; even worse, Sofia could feel her mother's sadness, loneliness, and she wished she could take her heartache away.

"Who does she want to love her?" Sofia asked Angelica kneeling beside her mother looking at her trying to read her.

"Your father," Angelica responded.

Sofia could not believe that her father, the man who once looked at her mother with profound love, makes her mother feel as though he does not. "He does love her," Sofia replied in an offensive tone jerking her head back at Angelica.

"It's not that he doesn't, my dear. He simply was not ready to be a father, and while the tradeoff was worth it for your mother; it wasn't the same for him." Angelica told her gently.

"I don't understand they are married," Sofia spoke puzzled. "How could he feel that I wasn't worth it?"

"Oh yes, he does eventually marry your mother, but it took him longer to understand that sacrifices must be made. He wasn't ready to give up his fun-filled life. Eventually, he did. When you are young, it's hard to look outside of your own wants and needs. It can be difficult for you to consider someone else, and what's best for them," Angelica explained.

"Mom did," Sofia quietly stated.

"Yes, she did," Angelica said softly. "It doesn't always happen. Sometimes the mother is ready. Sometimes, it's the father. Sometimes, it's neither. In this case your mother was ready;

however, being ready doesn't mean you're prepared."

"What do you mean?" Sofia asked.

Angelica slowly pointed back towards her mother, and when Sofia looked back, she watched her mother in different scenarios cry and pray the same prayer. Sofia's heart broke for her mother, as she understood what it felt like to question if someone loved her. She thought to herself that maybe her father didn't love her the way she thought. Maybe because she was born, it made him realize his true feelings for her mother, and it wasn't love.

Every day all her mother did, was hold her infant child in her arms, and wonder if she would ever be enough her. The sight was not easy to take, and the more she watched, the more sympathetic Sofia began to feel.

"So, when does God make him love her?" Sofia asked staring at her weeping mother. "When did He answer her prayers?"

Angelica snickered a little at her question, but responded with, "God, cannot force someone to love another. Each person can choose who they love. He provides everyone with the one He has planned for them, but often they choose not to accept and choose someone else. Or they accept them, but rush into a life with them before He has properly prepared them."

"So, was my father the right one, or the wrong one," Sofia questioned.

"That is not my place to know," Angelica replied.

"Well, if you end up with the wrong one how are you supposed to know. She obviously feels alone, how is she supposed to make it through until he decides he is ready?" Sofia asks frustratingly.

"While He cannot force someone to love another, or make their timing right, he can send her love through a gift," Angelica stated in a proverbial manner.

"How? What was the gift?" Sofia asks.

"You," replied Angelica.

Angelica smiled at her. She softly tucked her hair behind her ear, as her hand caressed her jawline coming to an end at her chin and said, "She had you to fill her days, to love on, and to play games. You gave her happiness, but the only way you can truly understand anything is if you see for yourself."

Sofia didn't understand, but she turned her attention back to her mother, and watched to see her mother's life play out.

Her mother sat and tossed out the papers to the military, because she couldn't fathom being away from her daughter. Giving up her dream, she held Sofia in her arms and sang to her. Her once dream was replaced with a new dream to be able to sing to her daughter every night for as long as time would allow. Her lullabies tapered off, as a new memory was played. Sofia watched her mother turn down a scholarship to college because it was in another state. There was no way she could raise her daughter without her support system. Her mother never blinked, she cradled her daughter in her arms, and said, "You're more important."

She could see in her mother's eyes that there was no where she would rather be. Sofia started to tear up, as she watched her mother give up her dreams for her. Her mother twirled in circles and as she spun around Sofia could see herself and her mom, age.

Then amidst their twirling there was a knock on the door, and it was a man. He had come to turn off their electricity because their bill had not been paid. Her mother gave the man, all the money she had to keep their lights on. You could tell she was sad, but when she turned back to her small child, she started to twirl again.

The next memory showed her mother entering a pawn shop, in the hopes of selling her jewelry. Sofia, looked confused, as her mother had pawned her only valuable necklace that was given to her by her grandmother, the one she said was the most beautiful she had ever seen. When given the money she sought out to buy clothes for her daughter. Upon returning home, they shared hugs and little Sofia was happy. Her mother received nothing, but she was covered in happiness, and regretted absolutely nothing.

They left the store and entered their old kitchen. Sofia could barely remember this house because she was so little. The kitchen was both the laundry room and the living room sort of combined, with the couch and tv on one side of the room, and the sink and washer and dryer on the other. She watched her mother cook food from their bare cabinets. When dinner was ready, Sofia watched as she ate, while her mother drank only a glass of water. Sofia got her tummy full, and had a bath, bedtime story, and was tucked safely in bed. Her mother took her plate and ate the few bites that were leftover and was oddly satisfied.

Sofia's heart was heavy, but of all the memories she watched, her heart was about to take a huge hit. Sofia watched her sick mother, unable to pick herself up left all alone. She had no one, all she had was a small child, who didn't understand what was happening. She cried in pain, when her head hurt, but there was no medication. She would fall over trying to make it to the kitchen to make meals for Sofia. But she never allowed her to go hungry.

Soon enough, the memories began to speed up, and Sofia watched her mother mend their clothes, because they couldn't afford more. She watched her make handmade decorations for birthday parties because store bought was expensive. She saw her break a dish and pay for a new one with change. She viewed every bit of her mother's life, and never once saw her mother receive anything in return. Most importantly her heart never saddened over anything. She was happy to sacrifice for her daughter.

As time progressed their father spent more time with them, while their struggles did not end, they were all together. Eventually her little sister Isabella was brought into the world. Their family was complete.

Sofia stood in a quiet stance, her heart sad, and her eyes burning. Standing there with no emotion to show, she assumed that she had cried so much, that she had no more tears to shed, and so she sat in regret. Sofia could see that times were hard, and in the beginning were not very happy. She also knew that as she had gotten older, she had not been thankful towards her mother. She had not shown her appreciation for all she had done for her. The longer she thought about her actions, she realized that during all these memories when her father was away, as she has gotten older, he was always around. He became prepared for the trade.

While her father grew to be a better person for her mother and her, she felt that she had become worse. She was no longer the sweet curly haired girl twirling around with her mother. Even worse, now she was the reason why her mother was sad. She and her father had switched places. Once again, another panic attack ensued, and she could feel her chest pounding. With every pump of blood, it ached more and more. When she started to feel the sensation of daggers piercing her chest, she had an epiphany.

She always thought her mother gave her a hard time because she wasn't perfect, but it's because she endured so many hardships in life and all she got in return was a mean teenager who lacked empathy. She concluded that all signs pointed to the fact that today, her mother regretted having her.

If her mother never would have had her, she would've had the future she planned on. Dad would've been ready when the time came, and she wouldn't have had to sacrifice for a selfish daughter. Upon this realization, her chest burned, and she spoke aloud, "I ruined her life."

"No, no, no. Don't you see, you made her life. You and your sister both," Angelica reminded her quickly. "No, she didn't receive her dreams, or accomplish her goals; but did you not notice that she never asked for anything, ever. She stripped herself from everything she had, to give back to you. Why do you think she did that?"

Angelica could not believe that she could create an interpretation such as that, but here she was fearing that she was a mistake. She could only hope that her explanation could help her comprehend the truth behind what she had seen. She stared waiting to hear what Sofia would say.

Sofia sat perplexed as she had not considered why her mother never asked for anything, and why she was always more than happy to go without. Looking at Angelica, she hoped for a good answer that would reason away her own explanation.

Angelica smiled longingly at her because she realized that her explanation was getting through. She decided Sofia needed to hear something more, and said, "Because she had already received gifts. You and your sister are all she needs. Seeing you happy, cared for, and loved was enough."

Sofia felt so loved by her mother. She never considered that her mother would think of her happiness as a gift. She felt guilty, but relieved. She wished for the first time in her life, that she *could* be the gift that her mother thought she was.

Feeling her chest pain subside, Sofia reached out to her mother's hand, as the room darkened, and she vanished. The only thing left to say was,

"I hope she knows how much I love her."

Sofia looked off into the darkness wondering what would be next, when a loud gong-like sound was heard. Stunned into silence, Angelica spoke a single sentence, that truly terrified her, "It's time."

# *Chapter 13*

Those words stopped every thought flying through her mind. It was if they were the magic words to permanently paralyze a person. With Angelica still holding out her hand, Sofia knew that there was nothing else left to do or say. She took her hand with great hesitation and then allowed Angelica to wrap her up in her soft glowing wings one last time.

She felt heavy in a way as if the sins she had committed had been morphed into weights and then strapped to her body. Worried and overly burdened, she wondered what would become of her. Will she enter the kingdom of heaven? Or will she suffer in the darkness of hell?

Angelica's wings were the last comfort she felt as she was carried away to what would be Sofia's death sentence. However, the safety she felt inside Angelica's wings, gave her a sense of hope. She knew that there was so much that happened, that even she couldn't decide where she should go. She was on a proverbial balancing beam and uncoordinated as she is, she didn't know if she would make it or fall.

After everything she had viewed, she couldn't positively say that she did anything to deserve the kingdom of Heaven. Please, let there be something to save me, she thought.

Soon, Angelica gently opened her wings and spoke softly to her, "Sofia."

Sofia didn't want to know the answer that had been decided and remained still with her eyes held tightly shut. Her little sister did this quite often when they would play hide-and-seek. While it didn't work for Isabella, she figured if she kept her eyes closed and was still, Angelica would feel sorry for her, and she wouldn't have to know.

Feeling Sofia's desperation Angelica placed her finger on the bottom of her chin, and gently raised it up towards her, watching a rolling river of tears roll down her face from her clenched eyes.

"Sofia, open your eyes," Angelica said. "It's okay."

Sofia slowly opened her eyes and seeing the calming and happy facial expression on Angelica's face, all she could feel was relief. Her face was lit with a warm light, and there was no feeling of fear around them. Sofia did not know if it was because she was still so close to Angelica or because they weren't in hell. She looked around and there was no fire, no demons, nothing that would suggest that hell is where she was. Filled with excitement she started to form a smile, because she figured if she wasn't in hell, then she must be in heaven.

"YE-," Sofia started to shout and jump before Angelica interrupted while she was in midair.

"Hold on," Angelica interrupted. "You're not in heaven, the decision has not been made yet."

Sofia was immediately confused and asked, "Where are we then?"

"We are waiting in the holding room," Angelica revealed. "This isn't a common thing, you see, it is typically easy to know where everyone should go, but your case is still being argued, at this time."

She suddenly remembered the glint of a hint of heaven that she got to see before their adventure took place and she realized, that while there were no signs of hell, there were also no signs of heaven either. There were no gates. There were no mansions. There was only the same white emptiness that surrounded her when she first started this journey. While she was happy that she hadn't been immediately sent to hell, this also greatly disappointed her. She wished she knew what the answer was going to be. The dramatic wait was killing her.

Slumping down by the weight of anticipation, she thought about those golden gates. To be able to see them open into the streets of gold would be one of the happiest times of her life. To experience the one thing that so many people describe as Home. She wondered if that feeling would ever be experienced for her.

Sofia felt the nerves kick in, and she had no idea how to resolve these emotions. She decided to think about everything she could have learned in hopes that maybe with the extra time, she'd be able to learn the lessons intended for her. She thought about Sarah, Isabella, and her mother. These were all people she had hurt, but in the moment, she felt that they were in the wrong. She sat along a white bench in their white room and questioned her own character.

Sofia had randomly bumped into a woman who had been beaten most likely every day of her life. She hurt her unknowingly, and then refused her the slightest kindness. Sarah's brutally assaulted body on the floor of her home flashed in her mind.

She verbally assaulted her five-year-old sister who only wanted to spend more time with her. All so she could be left alone to dwell in her own self-pity. Her mind then shifted to the image of her sister's future body lifeless on the floor of her bedroom.

As for her mother, she gave her everything she ever needed without a single word of regret. She treated her as Sam treated Sarah, thinking that being hateful and forceful were the only ways to get someone to see their side of the story. She instantly remembered the last look of her mother's face before their car was struck.

She felt horrible. She never tried to do better, to be better. She only tried to look at the picture in front of her, instead of the big picture.

The big picture was, each of these people desired love, and deserved love. She could have been the one to take time to say the right thing, to do the right thing, and to feel the right things. But she did not...

Sofia let out a tearful sob, and Angelica was intrigued. There was nothing in front of her, nothing was said, but for some reason, Sofia was weeping.

"What's wrong dear?" Angelica asked resting her hand on her shoulder.

Between sobs Sofia was able to answer, "I-I am a horrible person, aren't I?"

Angelica felt for her because it's hard for people to accept when they have done something wrong. She gave her a lengthy but well needed hug and answered her question.

"No one is perfect my love. We are all broken from the moment we are brought into the world, and it's through God, that we are able to be better. Not perfect but better. No one gets it right a hundred percent of the time. It only matters that they accept when they don't, to change what they can," Angelica stated.

Sofia lifted her head from Angelica's shoulder and recanted her last moments with her mother out loud and said, "The last words I spoke to my mother, was that I never wanted to speak to her again." Sofia had tears pouring down like rivers on her cheeks, absorbing into Angelica's hair. "I don't know what their judgement will be, but my judgement has been made; I am an awful person," she spoke.

Their hug progressed, with Angelica holding her a little tighter than before. When Angelica slowly pulled the two apart, and said, "Judgements are made by the fruits you bear, and by feeling guilty, you show remorse. By feeling sad, you show compassion. By shedding tears, you show sympathy. By wanting others to have better, you show love. These are fruits of our Lord. I think that there's a chance for you."

Sofia began to feel better and figured that maybe things will work out after all. Unfortunately, she would have to wait for the deliberation, and what if they didn't see what Angelica could see?

Sofia sat in deep thought about what her own future would hold, and she began to think again about the lives she affected that she would be leaving behind. Would Sarah have the courage or support system to ever leave her husband? Would her mother know how much she loves her? Would someone remind her sister how amazing she is, so she could fight?

Sofia's thoughts of her sister were interrupted by a dramatic thunder. The room began to shake, and rumble, and on the left side of the room there came the same sandstorm that once appeared before. It was the whitest sand she had ever seen, and through the grains Sofia could make out something transforming before her. She stood up in slow motion, watching the events taking place before her, and a door began to appear. It was a double door, with stained glass and gold edging. The picture held a white dove with an olive branch, sitting on what resembled an altar, and a breastplate with an axe. Surrounding the edge of the picture was twelve colorful squares. The trim around the doorway was decorated in angels and flowers. Sofia knew what this meant, but still she looked to Angelica for confirmation.

As Angelica smiled and gave her a subtle nod, they slowly came together. As both the doors appeared it was clear that oddly enough, both Sofia and Angelica were searching for courage to open the doors. Sofia needed courage because she was afraid of the answer they would give. Angelica needed courage not for herself, but for Sofia. She had grown quite fond of her, and she could not have been prouder of her as her guardian angel with the progress she had made throughout their destinations.

Relinquishing her planted feet, Angelica took the first step towards the door, but Sofia stayed planted in her place frozen as if the ice waters of the Atlantic Ocean had poured over her and turned her into ice. While she stood in awe of what had occurred before her very eyes, as she had never seen such a remarkable sight. She remained still scared to death about the outcome of what lie behind those doors, for what lie past them was the decision of all decisions. Trying to uproot her feet, she had to escape her thoughts, but all that did was remind her of the last thought she had just before the doors had appeared. Her sister's face filled her mind.

"What's wrong, love?" Angelica asked quizzically.

Sofia knew exactly what she needed in order to make it through those doors to accept her fate. No matter what the outcome may be, she would walk through them and accept accountability. She only needed to ask one simple question; she just didn't realize how difficult it would be to ask it.

Desperately desiring to know, she breathed in and...

"Before we go in, just tell me," Sofia said then taking in a deep breath once again. She said, "I understand that I hurt a lot of people through my actions, and I know that I will never be able to take any bit of it back in my lifetime. But. I cannot walk through that door without one last lesson."

Angelica was now confused, for Sofia had created another lesson, but what could it be?

Sofia looked straight ahead at the doors in front of her and asked the only question she had left. She asked, "If this whole accident could have been prevented, and I lived... Would I have been a compatible donor for my sister?"

Amazed at her question because she didn't know how to answer. For the first time during their journey, Angelica was the one to cry uncontrollably. How was she supposed to answer such a question? She grasped her hand tightly as she started to speak but fumbled over the words.

"That's difficult to answer. I-I... I-I don't quite know what to say."

Sofia stood permanently still, as the only thing that would release her from her place would be the answer to her last question.

Angelica took just a second and gathered her strength. Through her sobbing, she stared at Sofia who refused to remove her eyes from the doors, and she said, "Yes, my dear. You were."

# *Chapter 14*

The impact of those words was like being struck by that semi over again. Sofia's eyes closed in utter heartbreak. That one last lesson was the last nail to her coffin, as she felt completely shattered from her experience. Opening her eyes back up, she gave a slight nod, and she was ready to accept her fate.

Whoever was on the other side of those doors, must have known what Sofia had been waiting on, because once she had given the nod they opened. As they stood there the light shone in toward them and nearly blinded Sofia. Scared to take the first step, she started walking forward trustingly following Angelica's lead as she led her in. Angelica had not steered her wrong yet, why would she start now.

The further they entered the less the light shined. Sofia was able to make out small images of what was around her. There were shelves of some sort, or maybe desks. She couldn't definitively say what the objects were, but soon she sees something else.

Nearing a stopping point she sees Angelica beside her, motioning for her to take a step up. She stands on a platform with a podium in front of her. Unsure of what will happen, she remains focused on what she sees just beyond the platform of which she stands.

Stretching her sight out, she could make out twelve silhouettes, but their faces were not yet revealed. Who were they, and what would they have to say about her? She thought there would only be one person making the decision, but now there were twelve. When the light finally lessened to allow for Sofia to see clearly, what lie before her was something greater than she'd ever known.

There before her stood the twelve disciples of Jesus, and behind them standing tall and captivating, was the golden gates of heaven. There was nothing more beautiful or breath-taking. She couldn't believe she was just footsteps away for something she had only read about. Her eyes looked intently down the gates, until her gaze was upon the disciples.

Sofia looked at each remembering each of their stories from the Bible that she had learned every day of her life from Sunday school. Taking every second of information in, her quiet thoughts were cut short. When the first of the disciples made their first argument.

"Before any decision can be made, we must first look for ourselves not only of your life, but your heart during your life," Peter said.

They each closed their eyes, and silence filled the air. When each of their eyes opened with a golden light just the same as Angelica's once had. Not knowing what they were looking at, or what she should be doing, Sofia looked at Angelica for direction.

She motioned towards the floor, and Sofia looked down to see the floor change to clouds, that suddenly began to whirl around. They appeared to simulate the effects of a tornado accept, within the eye of the storm there was only her. She stood there ultimately watching every failure she had ever made.

After being taken to three different destinations, with three different people, Sofia looked at her past experiences and could see her sins plain and clear. She did not look at herself, thinking that her actions were justified. She looked at herself thinking how she wished she could go back and do something different.

They watched her cuss at people, they watched her steal. They watched her lie. In every scenario, you could tell that Sofia did not feel guilty.

Thinking that this would be all they based their decisions on, they began to look at her journey with Angelica. With each end of each destination, you could tell that there were lessons being learned. There was guilt, remorse, empathy, and compassion being learned. You could tell that Sofia had a good heart.

The images slowly faded out and the clouds stopped swirling. They shifted lower and lower appearing almost flat until the floor returned to its previous state. Sofia closed her eyes in prayer, praying that they could see the goodness in her. That there would be something in her that they could see to help save her. Unfortunately, she came to know that her prayers had been rejected when the next disciple spoke.

"Absolutely not," Andrew stated. "She never felt remorse for anything she did, she only wanted to pass the blame."

James, son of Zebedee stated, "Excuse me, she said she didn't think anything was her fault, but when it came to her mother, she felt so guilty she had to check on her. That looks like remorse to me."

"James, just because you look back doesn't mean you have the Lord in your heart. Look at Lot's wife," Interjected John.

"Yes, but she has learned her lesson, and isn't that the most important part? Right, Peter?" Philip said looking directly at Peter, knowing his past.

Bartholomew jumped in, "Peter learned his lessons when he was alive, not after."

Each of the disciples fought back and forth making sense of Sofia's actions as well as her heart. The more they spoke the more they found reasons why Sofia should not enter the Kingdom of Heaven. Their arguments each made sense, because even though Sofia wanted to see the Kingdom of Heaven, she could not remove the pictures of Sarah, Isabella, or her mother out of her head.

She thought over the arguments they had made, and she knew they had a very valid point, she wasn't always a nice person. She didn't always do the right thing, and while she figured that some of these disciples had no room to talk, not pointing fingers…. Judas. She knew that we all must face the consequences sometime, and for her, that time was right now.

The fact that she could spend eternity in hell scared her, but surprisingly not as much as she thought. Why wasn't she terrified? Why wasn't she begging and pleading with them to change their minds? Then it hit her. She wasn't terrified because her horrors had already happened. She was about to be dead, not dying, dead. Her mother was going to be less a child. A child she had fought and sacrificed so much for.

She was more terrified for what her mother's life was going to be like, as well as her sisters'. She wished there was some way, that she could prevent them anymore pain. What was she to do?

As Sofia's thoughts raced, she could hear the continuous arguments being made, when finally, Angelica decided to jump in with her own argument.

"Excuse me," Angelica said loudly attempting to overpower their voices. "Sofia has made a lot of mistakes in her life, but we all know that no one is perfect," she said, staring at Judas with a long cold hard stare. "But I feel as though we have forgotten one of the greatest things seen from Sofia, and that was her realization that she was wrong. She felt sorry. She felt regret. She felt compassion for these people. Aren't these the emotions given by our Lord?"

"She also felt anger, hatred, selfishness, and denial. These are not the emotions of our Lord," Interrupted Matthew with James shaking his head in agreeance.

Sofia felt ashamed that their accusations were undeniable. She hung her head in shame. Looking at Sofia, Angelica decided to change her angle, and hit them all where it hurts the most.

"I was once a troubled youth, spouting sinful language, and hateful words. I was once an adulterer, a liar, a cheat. I don't think there was any sin I did not commit. It took a sickness for me to change my ways. A near death experience for me to realize that I wasn't living for the Lord, I was living for myself. I hated every day and found no joy in the seconds or years ahead; I was just living. Nearly dying allowed me to accept my faults, and I worked every day of the rest of my human life to find joy in every ounce of air I breathed. I made amends with the ones I hurt. I changed my ways, and I was able to see Heaven."

Hearing Angelica's speech of her past life, intrigued Sofia. She was once as broken as she was, and yet she found a way. They were a lot alike, and she couldn't help but think that maybe this was why Angelica was meant to be her guardian angel. With hope in her eyes as she gazed at Angelica unveiling her past to the twelve disciples desperately trying to stand up for Sofia, she listened intently to her last words.

"Her mother felt she was worth the sacrifice, just as Jesus did for you all," Angelica claimed after a moment of hesitation.

All the disciples were stumped in quizzical thought. Not only had they never had a guardian angel interrupt them when they spoke, but they had never had one bring them up into conversation. Let alone, bring their own past up for discussion. They each began to look back and forth at one another seeking for one of them to have some kind of rebuttal. Then almost simultaneously they each found something to say, and the room exploded with loud protruding voices.

Despite the loud argumentative statements from the disciples, Sofia looked over at Angelica and was thankful for her input. She found her attempt to save her eternal soul, heartfelt, touching, and quite revealing. However, as she could hear them argue, she stood in silence enjoying the beauty of the friendship she had found in her guardian angel. Then in an enlightened burst of peace she obtained a true moment of clarity, where she could see clear as glass. She knew what she wanted to do, but it was going to cost her. It was time for her to make her very first sacrifice.

Despite Angelica's hard-hitting argument, her last remark fueled another argument. Unfortunately, it did not appear to be in Sofia's favor, and she couldn't think of a better time to cut into the conversation.

"Excuse me," Sofia said but was unable to be heard as the disciples continued in conversation.

"HEY!" Sofia shouted scaring Angelica.

Appalled at her interruption, they all looked at her in shocking dismay and waited to hear what she had to say. Their look of disapproval deeply concerned Sofia, but she knew she needed to get this out.

"I just wanted to make you an offer," Sofia said awkwardly.

"An offer?" said James, son of Alphaeus.

"I want to sacrifice my eternal soul to hell, on one condition," Sofia suggested quickly as if she were ripping off a band-aid, hoping they would be intrigued enough to listen.

Thaddaeus answered her with a curious response, "Condition? What's the condition?"

Sofia closed her eyes to get a grip on her body that was shaking quite noticeably. All the attention from the disciples with their looks of disdain, made her question if she should have just let them send her to hell.

She remembered the stories, and she remembered the glint of Heaven that Angelica had shown her. She was nervous and started to sweat, which is something she didn't think could happen after you die. Nevertheless, she wiped her brow and closed her eyes, and remembered why this sacrifice needed to be made. With those she loved, and those she hurt weighing heavy on her heart, she opened her eyes to explain. Before she could speak, she could picture in her mind everything she would miss out on with this sacrifice, but knew it was going to be the right choice. The best choice. The only choice.

Sofia waited until their eyes were all focused on her, and she said, "To live again."

# *Chapter 15*

"LIVE AGAIN?" Peter said. "You want to spend eternity in hell, so you can do what? Cause more problems for people? Hurt more people?"

Half of the disciples began nodding their head in agreeance because, she was not proven to be a reliable person. What more should they expect from her? The other half didn't agree but they also didn't root for her. What she was asking didn't feel right, and from what they had seen, they would be taking a huge chance to for her to fail and miss out on Heaven completely.

Seeing that the disciples were all up in the air over her offer, she felt an insisting urge to clarify her intentions.

"No," Sofia replies. "I don't want to live my life out; I just want to go back to make things right."

The disciples sat there perplexed at what Sofia was asking, and they couldn't understand what she had in mind. She wanted to live again just to fix a few things. This type of negotiation made zero sense. Then out of the silence came a question.

"Please, child. Explain to us more thoroughly so we might understand exactly what you might have in mind," John stated.

Sofia prayed that she would be able to find the words to use, so that they might understand what she means. She whispered silently with eyes held tight, and when she could feel the words lining up to be spoken, she began her explanation.

"I understand that I was not always a nice person. I know that I didn't do right. I treated people poorly, and I left them broken. There were so many things that occurred around me, but I was always so focused on myself, that I couldn't see anything else, but me."

She could feel a lump in her throat build as she noticed her emotions beginning to get out of control. She knew she was in the wrong, but there was nothing she could do to take it back. She looked at each disciple in their eyes as she made her case. "I know you're leaning towards sending me to hell, and I do not blame you. I blame myself. I figure that if I have to go because I've done so much bad; then could I at least go back to do something good?" she asked.

They all looked at her some unsure of what was she was thinking. Would she honestly go back and correct her mistakes? Was she really willing to sacrifice the gloriousness that is Heaven, just to make things, right? The others could see the good in her, and the sincerity in her offer. She awaited their verdict, until someone asked one last question.

"What good will you do and how long do you intend to take to do it?" Judas asked shifting in his seat, appearing uncomfortable with his own statements. "We all make mistakes that we wish we could take back, but how do you think you can fix something that you already broke?"

Sofia knew the answer without hesitation. "When you break a vase, you will never be able to glue it back together and make it perfect again, because the cracks will always be there. However, you can still glue it, and take precautions so it never happens again."

The analogy didn't completely hit home with the disciples. She could tell because even Angelica, Miss analogy queen didn't look like she quite understood either.

"What I mean is…," Sofia spoke again to explain. "I am the one that broke them, and while those scars will always be there; I can do something to make it better, and make sure it doesn't happen again."

"How do you plan on doing that?" Simon asked.

Sofia made eye contact with each person before her, before she started to speak, making sure she had each of their full attention. She said, "I need to make things right. It won't take long, a few hours at the least. I need to apologize to Sarah, the woman I bumped into. Not because I bumped into her, but because I need her to know that I don't agree with her husband. She is beautiful, and a gift to this world. She needs to know that there's a strength in her to find a new road to her future. What she feels is not a feeling of God, and she can overcome." With that comment she glanced at Angelica, as she thought about her road analogy, and Angelica smiled in delight. She understood completely.

After their moment was shared, Sofia continued with her reasoning. She said, "I need to remind my sister that even though I can say hurtful things, I never mean them. I should never speak to her that way, and I do not deserve to have such a caring sister like her. She is and has always been my favorite person because she is the sweetest person I know.

From the moment she was born, she had my heart, and I knew then that I wanted her with me always. I will do anything for her, she can have anything of mine including my kidneys if it means saving her life."

Sofia was overwhelmed by the thought of losing her sister, that she couldn't contain her emotions. She began to weep. Losing the words, she breathed in and out until she was able to find the words again. A gentle touch from Angelica helped calm her, as it always does. She began again with her argument.

"I need to tell my mother that… she was and is my whole world. Everything I am, is because of her, and without her I am nothing. She was my light, in the darkness, and she was my saving grace when I felt like death surrounded me. She sacrificed everything for me because she thought I was worth it, and I need to tell her, thank you. Thank you for loving me each and every day. Every minute. Every hour. I did not deserve it, but I am so glad she did," Sofia said sobbing uncontrollably.

Getting herself under control, she proclaimed to the disciples, "I know it doesn't exactly make sense, I mean why would I ask for a few hours, only to spend eternity in hell. However, I don't think that is completely for you to understand, and I think it's something that only God himself could comprehend. But to put it simply. I'd rather spend eternity in hell knowing my family and the people I have hurt, know that I loved them, and they made my life beautiful and happy, than go to heaven knowing that they will forever be broken because of me. Angelica has taught me, that we have the opportunity of every second of every day to show people love. We do this through what we say, what we do, and how we respond. I robbed myself of those moments, and I can never get them back. But if given this opportunity, I will gift every second I have left to them."

Angelica could be seen a mile away as she appeared to be brighter than normal. Her smile was gleaming, and she was apparently excited that the rude girl she witnessed only a short while ago, who was determined to prove her problems were due to everyone else in her life, had bloomed. She blossomed into this incredibly selfless woman. She couldn't have been prouder of Sofia in this moment. She walked towards her and held her in her arms.

"I am so proud of you," Angelica told Sofia giving her a heartfelt hug.

They embraced each other, as they both could use some affection during this difficult time. Shortly after, they looked back at the disciples to see about their deliberation.

They all were whispering quietly to one another, not a single one raising their voice.

They were making a plan, and Sofia couldn't help but wish they were as loud as they were when they were arguing about her. Soon their deliberation came.

The room grew silent and there was tension in the air. Sofia couldn't tell which way they were going to go but prayed that they would choose the best outcome for her family and now friend, but also, for her too.

Peter stood while everyone else sat still, glaring into the eyes of Sofia. He said, "Sofia, never in all the history of man, have we received a person willing to negotiate their soul to the darkest depths of hell, to help others in need. Not only has this never occurred, but no one has also ever given a speech quite as beautiful as yours. You have shown a side to yourself that has not been seen throughout your past, nor during your time with Angelica. However, your past character leaves us puzzled if you would actually follow through with your words. To send you back, only to make those lives you mention worse, would be unthinkable. With being said, we have reached the verdict for your eternal life."

Sofia could feel the anticipation growing, as she held Angelica close. Her heart started beating rapidly and hard. The pounding could be felt in the front of her chest in back, as if it were beating so hard it was hitting both sides. Then she began to sweat with streams of perspiration falling from her temple. She started to feel weak, first at her knees, then even her head felt too heavy to hold. Then just before true panic set in, her body felt cold, and the shakes took over. She was scared. She almost felt as though her body was giving up little by little. So, she prayed for just one more chance. One single opportunity to make things right. She knew she could turn things around for the people she hurt, if only she was given one. Last. Chance.

Peter took a moment of pause, assuming for dramatic effect, and said, "and the verdict is…"

Taking deep swallows, Sofia opened her eyes and leaned in to hear more clearer in case something didn't go right. Angelica followed her lead, as she was just as curious.

Then before another word could be uttered… there were three chilling chimes.

# *Chapter 16*

Instantaneous to the moment that Peter was about to announce their verdict for Sofia's negotiations for her eternal soul, three loud chimes interrupted him. The chimes struck fear in her nerves which erased the other emotions contaminating her body. Even though the chimes allowed her to regain feeling in her body function. She was still concerned. She scanned the room, only to find questionable behavior occurring. Each of the disciples looked around as though they were shocked to hear such sounds. Their eyes widened with an expression of what resembled fear. Sofia wasn't sure what was happening, but their facial responses confused her. There was something happening that Sofia was unaware of. However, as she looked to Angelica for understanding, she realized that Angelica shared their same expression. What did this mean?

There was not a way Sofia could fully describe what emotions she was feeling, but she was left in a curious state. What was going on? What were they thinking? What did the chimes mean? Could this possibly mean that it was too late for her negotiation to be made? Did she just lose her only chance?

Every thought flooding her mind was lost with that last simple question. She looked at each one individually, and as they came to terms with the lingering chimes, their expressions changed from fear to something else. With her gaze investigating them intently, she felt she understood the reasoning behind their expressions, and it was one that she knew all too well. It was the expression one has when they are spoke to by someone they fear; but who could it be? Who do they fear?

Within seconds they began to lower their gaze back to her. They looked at her as though there was something drastic about to occur. Something so overwhelming that even they couldn't believe it. They looked at Sofia in disappointment, and sadness poured over them.

Sofia knew without a doubt in her mind, that whoever spoke to them, would not give her a second chance. There was nothing like experiencing the failure she was feeling right now. She just knew that she had ran out of time.

Her head sank and she started to cry. She couldn't believe she would never have that chance. The chance to change everything. Because of her everyone's life was going to go astray, and they would all be lost. She shook her head thinking of the stupid mistakes she had made all because of her selfishness. Angelica was right, she had been blinded all her life.

Peter spoke into the silence and said, "Sofia, the chosen twelve have deliberated about the location and negotiations about your soul. We determined that your desire to show others love, and place them before yourself, sacrificing the greatest gift our God has in store for each one of us, proves that you are a child of God. We believed that all you truly wanted was a chance to return and make things right, so that they may be able to live a life of true happiness and eventually receive their future gift of eternal life."

Sofia listened intently but was confused as to where this was going. It sounded positive, but she couldn't help but feel that there was a *but* coming at the end of this speech. Like everything else she's experienced, she didn't feel it was something that she was going to like to hear.

"Upon delivery of your verdict, of which we had decided to grant you your offer, God had spoken," Peter said.

Sofia smiled and jumped in delight over the sweet words that just echoed in her ears. Thankful that they would give her this opportunity, she was taken aback by an interruption that ultimately decided her fate. Curiosity set in, with a punch of reality and she began to pray that God felt the same way His disciples did, but she feared maybe He didn't.

"Angelica, as you have watched Sofia throughout her life, caring for her, guiding her, and ultimately teaching her through her previous lessons, we shall disperse so that you may deliver her the decision made by God Himself," Peter said.

With a bow of his head, each of the twelve disciples stood in unison and their bodies were turned into a vapor. At the same time, the floors reverted to clouds, except this time they rose higher and higher covering the room around them. The only thing seen were twelve bright lights shining, that grew wider and wider until they touched each other, turning into one single light. Too bright to see, Sofia's instincts forced her to close her eyes. In seconds, all remanence of the room where she stood in deliberation were swallowed. When Sofia opened her eyes, all that was left was her and Angelica. They were back into the white room and the romantic stain glass doors were gone.

Hesitantly looking to Angelica for answers, Sofia saw that Angelica was not overjoyed to receive the responsibility of delivering the news. Her once perky personality had disappeared with the rest of the contents of the room. She was visibly choked up unable to get the first words out. Sofia knew that they had grown in their relationship, and she wanted to ease the pain for her newfound friend.

Sofia hugged Angelica so tightly, and gently whispered to her. "It's okay. I can accept my consequences. You don't have to be scared for me. I will be fine. With the option I gave them, hell was going to happen no matter what. Thank you for all you have done for me. You're amazing, and I pray that my sister has an Angel just like you."

They were both in tears, and Angelica returned her hug with such appreciation. As their hug came to an end, Angelica spoke to her between sobs, "I'm not scared for you, I am happy for what is happening for you. This decision can only help you, but…my heart is filled with sadness for you."

Angelica's comment made no sense. Sofia couldn't understand how she could be both happy, and sad. "What do you mean?" Sofia asked.

"God has spoken and has told us that a sacrifice has been made on your behalf. You will return home to your family and live out your days until your time comes again," Angelica told her with great happiness. "You have been given the second chance you prayed for."

Beyond excited Sofia was overcome with relief, joy, and utter disbelief. She was granted life. A chance to make things better for what she had broken and who she had broken. More importantly, a chance to save the lives of those she loved, and a chance to save her own. She would live again.

In hopeful tears, she cried out to God on bended knee, "Thank you. I am undeserving. You are merciful, and I pray Father that I prove my worth, my devotion, and my love for you. I will spread your word for as long as I live. I pray that everyone I encounter sees you in me. Thank you, Thank you!"

Sofia leapt back up in excitement and she started to think of all the ways she could make things better.

"OH, MY GOODNESS! I know what to do! I'm going to call every doctor and nurse in so they can go ahead and test Isabella. What if she already has it? I got to move fast. How long does it take to remove a kidney? Never mind, I'll do an internet search as soon as I get home," Sofia said, suddenly waving her arms around. "No, no, that would be bad. It doesn't matter, I just got to make sure they give her mine. Oh, and then I need to see my mom, she really needs to know how sorry I am. There was no excuse for my behavior. WAIT! There's Sarah, how am I going to find Sarah. I know what the inside of her house looks like but not the outside. I don't even know where it is. This is not going to be easy, but I don't care, I will find a way."

Angelica looked at Sofia with her expression becoming happier and happier, because Sofia was ranting just like Angelica, and it was refreshing. Noticing that Angelica was taking enjoyment out of her over the top scene, she paused on her list and just enjoyed this moment with her friend.

With a knowing look the room was filled with joyous praise, and laughter. Sofia and Angelica took the moment to dance, jump, and scream in excitement, but then…

Sofia's happy occasion was darkened by a sudden strike of memory. She was so thrilled by God's ruling, that she disregarded the rest of what Angelica had to say. Angelica had said she was happy, but she was sad. Why would she be sad? Then in an instant she remembered Angelica's words.

*A sacrifice has been made for you.*

These words filled her mind, and she couldn't help but wonder what sacrifice was made. Ending their joyous occasion, she turned to Angelica and looked for the answer but was afraid of what she may hear.

"Angelica," She asked building up courage to finish her question. "The sacrifice. What sacrifice was made, so that I could live?"

Angelica's face quickly changed from one of happiness, to one that was covered in grimness. She lowered her arms from their celebratory mood and took a few steps towards her. She placed her hands on Sofia's shoulders to brace her for her answer.

"A sacrifice of love," Angelica said gently.

"Sacrifice of love?" Sofia questioned.

A loud rumble was heard, that reverberated around them. A wind could be felt coming in from the left side. Just beyond Angelica, the white emptiness turned to clouds. Angelica's look glared up, and she said, "It's time to return."

Sofia starts to feel her body turn from warm, to empty. It was as though her body was fading away, and she couldn't stop it. The clouds around them were getting closer, and it was getting difficult to see. She looked down at her hands, and they were nearly see-through. Looking towards, Angelica, she could feel a tear leave her eye. Angelica released her hands from her, and said, "It's okay, I will see you soon."

As Sofia's body disappeared into the cloudiness, she could see something in the distance. She couldn't make it out, but she could feel a sense of love.

She strains her eyes to make out the figure, and just as the fading reaches her chest, she can see exactly who it is… it's her mother.

# *Chapter 17*

Vanished. She had vanished into the air. When the faint melody of a chime beeping in consistent repetition protruded into her conscious. Her senses heightened to discern the difference between where she was and where she might be now. She can feel the weight of her body, and the warmth of the blood running through her veins. She can feel her eardrums ache from the ringing of the chimes echoing in her ears. Her chest feels as though it is on fire, as the pain comes in waves. She realizes…she's asleep.

Finding the strength to open her eyes, she finds it's not as easy as anticipated. The first attempt only allowed her to shift her eyes. The second, allowed her to lift them enough to have the light shine into her pupils striking them with a vicious sting. Her final attempt resulted in her dramatically moving her eyes from one side to the other, which apparently meant shifting her head as well. Her dramatic flair worked, as she was finally able to open her eyes slowly as to not be blinded again. She awakens in a place unfamiliar. Her vision is blurry, and it's hard to make out certain aspects of what is around her. She was scared.

Struggling to breathe she can feel something lodged in her throat. Moving her arm to alleviate the clog, she feels a sharp pull on her hand. Her arms feel tied back, and she cannot seem to save herself from choking. Tears start to well, as she is in terror due to the confusing events, until she hears multiple voices shouting around her. Shocked she looks around and she can see their blurred silhouettes become detailed as they move closer to her. She didn't know what to be more worried about, the fact that she couldn't move or breathe, or that standing above her were doctors, and nurses.

"Calm down, sweetie. You're going to be okay," says a nurse. "Please don't move anymore, we need to remove your tube."

Panicked and afraid, Sofia didn't know what they meant. She had no idea what they wanted to remove or what they were talking about. She laid still just as they asked. Gently they removed a plastic tube that rubbed her throat as it made its way out. Once out she gasped for her first breath, and she was able to breathe on her own again.

Finally, without the restriction forcing her to keep her head still, she was able to take in the world around her. She looked to the left, at the monitors and then turned towards the right, to see the fluids for her IV going into her hand. She looked around adding everything up, but what worried her most was she couldn't hear what the doctors had to say. Their voices only sounded as softened hymns in her head. She knew they weren't singing, and whatever they had to discuss involved her. She started to lift herself up for a better earshot.

Seeing her moving into a sitting position she noticed them rushing toward her with a doctor on one side, and a nurse on the other. They urged her to remain still and lie down. Leaning back and closing her eyes, she remembered each of the events that had taken place. She remembered the mall, and Sarah. She recounted her sister and the words she left her with. She felt the pain of the accident. She replayed her adventure with Angelica and the lessons she learned. Most importantly she remembered, her mother.

Every image that fled through her mind, filled her with a power to remain true to her word. She was not going to go back on what she said. She was given this opportunity and she was going to take advantage of it. First, she needed to see her family, and it needed to happen now. She took in as much air as her lungs would allow, and resting her hand on the doctor's hand, she asked for one simple thing, "Bring my family to me, please."

Each person in the room looked to one another, as the doctor ordered the interns to get them immediately. She waited as they checked her to make sure she was doing well. Sofia could feel the anticipation growing, because she knew that she was ready to make this life count.

While the minutes felt like years, her family finally makes it to her, bursting through her room in complete excitement to know that she is okay. Her father enters with Isabella on his hip, and they're screaming. She can feel their love for her fill the room, and they all begin to cry. The initial sight of Isabella engulfed Sofia; her time was now. With Isabella sitting at the foot of her bed, her father stands right beside her and takes her hand. The doctors and nurses walk towards the back wall to give the family some room.

Her father bends over to give Sofia a kiss on her forehead, and then bringing his head to hers says, "I thought we lost you. I couldn't take that. Thank you for being strong enough to come back to me."

They take a moment feeling their father-daughter bond, ánd Sofia softly says to him, "I love you, dad."

Watching her sister and father have their moment, Isabella is overrun with emotions, and she begins to cry as well. Seeing her sister is a scary sight to see, and she doesn't know what to think. Sofia looks to her sister's tear-filled eyes, and tells her, "Hey, come sit a little closer to me here. Please."

Isabella begins making her way to Sofia, but almost falls off the bed, so their father steps in and helps. Mostly so Isabella doesn't fall, but also so she doesn't accidentally hurt Sofia in the process of sitting so close. Sensing her father's concern, Sofia finds the button to raise herself up and finds the perfect height to speak to her sister, so her father does not worry.

"Listen to me. Are you listening?" Sofia asks taking her hands in hers and staring straight into her eyes.

Isabella nods her head and waits.

"I know that I have not always been the best sister to you, but I want you to know that what I said to you was a lie," Sofia said, tears immediately rolling down her face. Their father looked at his daughters confused by the conversation. He listens intently to what his daughter has to say.

"I know you're only five, so we haven't had many years together, but you are still one of the best things in my life. You're not a brat. I know how strong you are, and funny, kind, smart. The day you were born I felt so blessed, because I would have a best friend for the rest of my life. I am so sorry; I acted the way I did. I never want you to feel like you're not worth having around. I need you to know, that I will always want you around. Please know, that I want you around, Isabella. I hope one day you can forgive me," Sofia said fighting the urge to let all her sorrows loose.

"I love you, Isabella. There's no better sister, than you."

"I love you too, Soso." Isabella said, referring to her with her favorite nickname.

Everyone in the room can feel the wave of emotion flood their hearts. They watch as the three of them hug each other tightly. Their love is so strong that nothing could invade the moment they were sharing. Pulling away from each other, Sofia was relieved that she was able to make things right with her sister. Feeling excited to move on to the next person, Sofia felt something strange. Shifting her look at her father he could sense something was about to steal the happiness in the room. Both Sofia and her father could feel a void in the air, but only he knew why. Sofia looked at the two of them, and looked around the faces in the room, and realized that her mother was not accounted for. She was so excited for the opportunity to make things right with her sister that she didn't realize that her mother was not with them. She must still be in her own room she thought.

Smiling happily, she asked her father, "Where's mom?"

There was nothing that could describe the looks that fell upon their faces. A look so grim that it sent chills down your spine and left a stinging pain in your heart. Sofia's happy smile turned into a whimpering frown. She could sense there was something bad happening, but she was afraid to examine it any further.

Seeing Sofia begin to shake, the nurse draws near. Sofia remembered her from when she had first entered the hospital, and her words echoed in her head. The nurse tenderly sat upon her bedside faintly disturbing the silence and breathed a heavy breath. She cleared the lump in her throat, looked to her father for confirmation and began her explanation. She said, "Sofia when you were brought in, your mother was brought in as well. You both appeared to be in bad shape, unfortunately you were in worse condition than your mother. Your mother sustained internal damage and needed surgery. You were pulled from the vehicle with a shard of glass piercing your chest, and it was likely that you would not make it."

She takes a pause, giving Sofia time to take in the information given, and when she appeared ready to hear more, she began again. "As we worked on your mother, she had asked one thing. She asked that you be saved even if it meant losing her. She made me promise."

Swallowing hard she continued, "Your mother came out of surgery fine. The internal bleeding was caused by a laceration of her kidney but through surgery we were able to fix it quickly before it was too late. Everything appeared to be a success; however, you were a different story."

The silence in the room was eerie, but Sofia wasn't about to break the silence, she needed to know where her mother was. She listened earnestly to her nurse. "You were in and out, from the moment you were retrieved from the crash. When you got here, we were worried you wouldn't make it. We rushed you into surgery, but the glass had pierced your heart. You died on the table three times. The last time we were able to save you, we weren't even certain that you would survive," the nurse said through tears.

Hearing the nurse tell Sofia that she had died three times struck her memory. She recalled the feeling of pain in her chest. She felt it three times, and every time it had lessened.

Those were the times she had died. She was completely shocked, that while she was living out lessons with Angelica, she was still feeling her own physical body. She turned her attention back towards the nurse, who finished the explanation with, "The next morning your heart ruptured, and you had to be taken to surgery immediately. There was a very small chance you would've survived another surgery to your heart."

Looking back to the doctors, and back at Sofia, the nurse eased her way into the last of her explanation. "At the same time of your surgery, your mother suffered an embolism that traveled to her brain, and…," the nurse searched for strength to finish her last sentiments.

"She died, before anyone could make it to her. There was nothing anyone could do." The nurse said, crying uncontrollably.

Sofia sat in disbelief. Her mother had died. She didn't understand, Angelica told her she was safe. Desperately looking for something to make sense, her doctor led the nurse from her bedside. He took his turn and sat at her bedside and began his explanation. He told her, "There's something else."

He gave her a folded piece of paper, and an envelope. The envelope had her name written on it, in her mother's handwriting. The papers were filled with information that she couldn't understand. Seeing her confusion, the doctor explained. "I don't know how your mother thought to fill these papers out before hand, but her last wish was that if something were to happen to her, we were to make sure your life was spared."

The doctor looked to see if she was grasping any of this information, and said, "Your mother was an organ donor, she asked that her heart be given to you. You're alive now because of your mother's sacrifice for you."

The moment the words left his lips, Sofia remembered what Angelica had told her.

*A sacrifice of love.*

Sofia cried like she had never done before holding the papers showing her mother's never-ending love. She felt pain, anguish, love, and it was too much for her to feel. She thought to herself as she opened the envelope, she gave her own life, so I could live.

Nervously pulling out the letter, she almost wasn't sure if she should open it, but she needed to know what her mother's last words to her were.

The letter wasn't long, it simply read:

"You're mine, and I am yours. There's nothing I wouldn't give for you. Until my last days, until my last breath, I will sacrifice my life for you."

# *Chapter 18*

Reading her mother's heart felt note, she thought of the life her mother held. Sofia had witnessed her mother endure so much heartache, struggle to get through, and all she ever wanted was her to know she loved her. Even though Sofia was ready to make amends and prove to her mother that she loved her more than anything, she realized that she could never take back those last words she said to her. Those words radiated through her mind hearing her mother's voice say, *"one day you will want to talk, but I won't be there."*

She was right. All she wanted was to talk to her, apologize to her, to tell her how amazing her life was because of her. She fell into a dark abyss in her mind thinking of the last moment where she made her mother feel unwanted, unimportant, and unloved.

Seeing her in pain as she read her note from her mother, Sofia's father reached in to hold her. Picking her head up softly and placing his arm around her, he laid beside her. Sofia unable to bear any more information, cried as she prayed in her father's arms.

*Father, I pray that mom has made it safely home, and that she knows how much I love her. I wish I had one last chance to tell her I'm sorry, and to hug her so she can feel the love I have for her. I pray she knows, and I'm sorry I couldn't keep my promise. In Jesus name, Amen.*

Almost instinctively knowing what his daughter must have prayed, he simply responded to his daughter, "She knows my dear. She's always known."

Hearing those words from her father, gave her hope. Even though she might have missed the opportunity to tell her herself, there was a chance that she had always known. She cried in her father's arms, wishing his comfort would ease the pain. She cried until she fell asleep. She cried…even in her dreams.

As the day pressed on, Sofia found herself waking from a deep sleep. She didn't know if it was morning or night, but she knew more than anything she needed that rest. The whirlwind of the day completely exhausted her. The crowd of people had dispersed from her room, and the emptiness allowed her time to recoup. Enjoying the silence, she heard footsteps nearing. Suddenly, the curtain was pulled back and it was a nurse but not the same as before. The shifts must have changed. She began writing something on the board, and then proceeded to walk over to her bed. Seeing Sofia awake, she said, "Hi honey. It is so good to see you doing better."

Sofia found a resemblance in this woman but couldn't place her at all. Her brown hair was pinned back, and she had a mask on that covered most of her face. All that could be seen was her eyes. She stared at her, as she checked her vitals hoping it would ring some bells. Was it the way her hair was styled that reminded her of someone? Was it the smell of her perfume? She thought and thought, but nothing. She couldn't put her finger on it, but there was something vaguely familiar. She closed her eyes briefly to find the connection between the two of them, hoping the answer would be found in the darkest parts of her memory.

The nurse began adjusting her wires as they were a bit tangled from her sleep, that she accidently pulled too hard. "Ow!" said Sofia.

"I'm so sorry!" the nurse apologized; and that's when it hit her.

Those words, *I'm sorry,* were like a lightning bolt into her mind. Everything erupted with certainty that those words were the ones that she heard that frightened her to the core. She knew exactly who she was, and the connection was certain.

"I know you," Sofia says, ignoring her apology.

"Well, I have been taking care of you, during the night but this is the first time we've met face to face." The nurse explains.

"No, you were there the day of my accident. You were in the mall," Sofia reminds her.

"Umm, well yes actually," the nurse responds curious as to how she knew. "I was there but I was inside the mall when it happened. Such a horrible accident. I'm so sorry for your loss."

The nurse lowers her head in grief, and Sofia replies, "No, I'm sorry for yours."

"Excuse me?" she asks in a puzzling tone. "Sorry for what? I haven't lost anyone."

Sofia could tell that she was sort of scaring Sarah, and if she didn't hurry up and get this out, she would have a new nurse during this shift. She spit it out as fast as she could.

"You've lost yourself."

Sarah's eyes nearly hollowed, as she waited to hear what else she had to say.

"Sarah, I'm sorry that I bumped into you, in the mall. I wasn't paying attention and I should have apologized. I was being selfish, and at the time, I didn't care; but I should have," Sofia said looking into the depths of her dark brown eyes. "I was upset, and unfortunately, I always seem to blame everyone else around me for my mistakes. I want you to always remember the words my mother told you. Sarah, you are important, you're not worthless. You are a wonderful person, and I am merely a rude and inconsiderate child, who should've taken a few moments to acknowledge your presence. I realize I hurt you, and I am sorry."

Sarah looked down in awe as she remembered the girl who bumped into her and made her feel worthless. She could picture her face looking at her with disdain. As she listens, Sofia is unsure of what she might do. Sarah, dropping her medical tools, grabbed her hands and starts to cry because the sound of an apology filled her body with encouragement. She felt seen.

"Thank you," she replied in tearful happiness. "Thank you so much for your kindness. You didn't hurt me; I was hurting long before you. I appreciate you taking the time to say such sweet words to me. No one has ever done that before, except of course, your mother."

Sofia placed her hand on top of hers and asked her to have a seat. She told her, "Please tell me anything you'd like to talk about. I know you have a lot on your heart, but before you say anything, can I just say… You are worth more than a man who'd hurt you, to save himself. He is not worth the sacrifice of your life for his."

Sarah's jaw dropped in astonishment and sensed that Sofia knew so much about her, but how? Even though she was a little frightened by her intimate details of her life, she had a calmness wash over her. The fact she knew so much about her made her realize that it didn't matter. She was relieved she had someone to talk to. Their conversation grew, and they laughed and cried until Sarah could feel a power within herself.

They spoke of how long she endured such a marriage due to the fact that they got married at such a young age. They married shortly after she obtained her RN license. She claimed he was kind in the beginning, and then by the night fall of their wedding, he struck her for the first time. He immediately apologized and claimed it was the alcohol from the reception. Over time he would have these instances more often, slowly merging closer and closer. The more often they occurred, the worse the beatings got. Before she knew it, she was ten years into their marriage, and she had nothing left to give. She sat in defeated posture, recalling how many times she begged for death. During this conversation, Sarah felt so close to

Sofia because she had never been able to be vulnerable with anyone.

Sarah and Sofia spoke of options for her to take, and she even offered up their home for her until she got on her feet.

Sarah was so thankful that she had a chance to speak to Sofia. She felt as though she was a wonderfully remarkable person, but she had some questions.

"Sofia," she asked after waiting for the right moment. "How did you know my name? I never gave it to you. Also, how did you know about my husband, I have never told a soul?"

Sofia smiled at Sarah's curiosity because she thought of a red-headed woman who opened her eyes to what she had been blinded from for so long. Thinking of the right words to explain, her eyes diverted to a speck that flashed behind Sarah. Just in the background, the speck grew wider, and brighter. Confused by what captivated Sofia, Sarah turned back to look as well, but nothing could be seen except the hospital wall. Staring intently Sofia could make out an image of something she had never been able to see. The image became golden and more detailed. It was the image of two people standing there together. She couldn't mistake them for anyone else. It was Angelica and her mother. Her heart pounded and she cried happily to see that her mother was with Angelica, and wouldn't you know it. Her mother had the most beautiful wings too.

Sofia softly whispered, "I'm sorry."

With a bright loving smile, her mother mouthed the words, "It's okay my darling. I love you too."

With that she found that finally her head and her heart were aligned, but only for a moment, because then they disappeared.

Shifting her stare back at Sarah, who was turning back around to check on her. Sofia found that there was only one way to possibly explain how she was able to know everything about her.

With the happiest of grins she said, "I know about you, because an infuriating, ball-busting, sweet, red-headed angel, showed me to save my life. If it wasn't for her and… my mother, I'd still be the selfish blinded person I was."

"Well, thank them for me, because now you're saving mine," Sarah claimed.

# *Chapter 19*

The two of them sat laughing and reminiscing, as Sofia decided to tell Sarah all about her experience during her death. However, interrupting their intensifying conversation they heard a knock on the door. Sofia's father and sister entered, and a wave of intense laughter came through the door. He couldn't decipher what two strangers would have so much to talk about, let alone joke about. He was eager to understand the happiness flowing from the room. Looking at the two on the bed, he was intrigued to know who they were they talking about? Also, what journey are they referring? He greatly wished to know the details in the conversation that held them captivated.

"What's going on here?" He asked.

"Nothing," Responded Sarah. "We're just having a little enlightening conversation."

"Enlightening conversation, huh?" Sofia's dad repeated.

Reading the room, Sarah decided that it was time for her to check her other patients. She figured she had spent way too much time tending to her when she had other patients to consider. With a heartfelt goodbye and hug, she attempted to leave the room, before she stopped at the door.

"Thank you for your offer, Sofia, but I know exactly where I can go," she said.

"Just as long as you remember I am always here for you. No matter where you go... just don't go back there," Sofia replied.

"Offer what?" her father questioned.

Giving each other a kind smile, Sarah returned to work. Even though their time together seemed to be helpful for them both, their last words weighed heavy on Sofia's father. Thinking deeply, he slowly turned his attention back to his daughter and made his way to her.

Sofia's father takes Isabella and sets her on Sofia's bed, and he takes a seat in the chair beside her. Pulling it closer to her, he finds a comfortable spot to begin his question. He asks, "So, do you mind telling me what just happened?"

Sofia could tell that her father's intuition was correct as something had indeed occurred between the two. However, instead of explaining Sarah's horrific life to her father, she decided to give him one of Angelica's philosophical explanations.

"Nothing, we simply needed to open our hearts to one another, and get closer. Sometimes it's better to talk than to keep things bottled up. After all, you never know what someone else is going through, until you take the opportunity to ask," Sofia explained.

Absolutely taken aback her father couldn't believe what his fourteen-year-old daughter has just said. Forgetting all questions that previously occupied his mind, he was unable to hold back the words about to spew from his mouth. He immediately asked, "Since when did you start talking like that?"

"Yeah, you sound like mommy," Isabella proclaims.

They laugh together at the silliness of Isabella's remark and take the time to remember their mother fondly. As they sit in remembrance their father expresses a simple thought, "I am so glad we got to keep you. You are a little piece of your mother."

Sofia had never thought of herself to have any characteristics that resembled her mother, mostly because she looked like her father. With being said, to hear her father utter those words made her so proud that he could see her that way. With that sentiment, Sofia smiled.

"You know, not many people get a second chance darling. What are you going to do with yours?" he asked her in curiosity.

Sofia thought of how she was going to use her second chance. What would she do? She had already done the things that she had promised. She thought and thought but only two things came to mind so far. She already knew that her character, attitude, and heart had changed, but the longer her thoughts dragged out, the more clarity she obtained. The two things she thought of, were the only things that mattered.

Smiling at her father a twinkle could be seen in her eye. She said, "There's two things that I am going to do. The first will forever remind me of mom's sacrifice for me."

How could someone recreate what her mother did for her? He thought to himself. Her mother gave her the heart from her chest to save her life. Wouldn't the scar alone remind her of that?

"How do you plan on doing that?" He asked with a hint of anticipation.

"I'm going to love. Love the way my mother loved me," she said bringing joy to her father's heart.

Her father was brought to tears because he had never heard Sofia speak like that, and the fact that she wanted to do something so kind and compassionate, reminded him of his dearly departed wife. That was something, only she would say.

"I cannot think of any other way to live. What a beautiful heart you have," her father said adoringly. "Afterall, it is your mother's."

There was nothing like the close feeling within a family, that made people excited about each other, and about life. Thinking of her mother, she thought of how she might be able to fulfill the dreams her mother once held. She and her father began thinking of ways to do good in the world, and he was more than happy to be by her side every step of the way. The longer she talked the more he saw her mother in her, and for a moment they both could feel her in the room.

As they locked eyes, her sweet sister Isabella spoke aloud, "But you said there were two things," she said confused and crossing her arms.

"Oh yes, you did," her father added. "I'm sorry dear, what's the other thing?"

Sofia turned her attention to her sister and smiled at her longingly. She reached out to her to come closer and cupped her hands around Isabella's face. With anticipation growing immensely for all of them, she pulled her face in close to hers. With their heads touching she spoke to her in a whisper and said, "The second thing involves you."

Pulling away, Isabella scrunched her nose, and wondered what her sister would do with her?

"Me?" She spoke inquisitively. "Are you going to give me something?"
Amazed at the wording of her question, Sofia giggled and said, "Yes. I have something very special for you."


THE END.